LAMENT AT
LOON LAKE

FAKES, FOLK MUSIC, AND GHOST FIRES

When legendary folk singer Lara Fairplay
agrees to make her comeback debut at
Pirate's Cove's annual maritime music festival,
everyone in the quaint seaside village
is delighted—including mystery bookstore owner
and sometimes amateur sleuth, Ellery Page.

Better yet, Lara is scheduled to perform
a recently discovered piece of music
attributed to "The Father of American Music,"
Stephen Foster, which will hopefully bring large
crowds and a lot of business.

Several mysterious accidents later,
Ellery is less delighted as his suspicion grows
that someone plans to silence
the celebrity songbird forever.

LAMENT AT
LOON LAKE

SECRETS & SCRABBLE BOOK SIX

JOSH LANYON

VELLICHOR BOOKS

An imprint of JustJoshin Publishing, Inc.

LAMENT AT LOON LANDING: AN M/M COZY MYSTERY
(Secrets and Scrabble 6)
May 2023
Copyright (c) 2023 by Josh Lanyon
Edited by Jennifer Jacobson
Cover and book design by Kevin Burton Smith
All rights reserved

Published in the United States of America

JustJoshin Publishing, Inc.
3053 Rancho Vista Blvd.
Suite 116
Palmdale, CA 93551
www.joshlanyon.com

This is a work of fiction. Any resemblance to persons living or dead is entirely coincidental.

To those honorary citizens of Pirate's Cove;
the readers who waited so faithfully,
so patiently for this long-delayed voyage.

Walk the plank and kiss the shark.

–Barry Dennis Hopkins

CHAPTER ONE

Whoooo.... Whooooo.... WHOOOOO!

Ghostly wailings seemed to issue from the blackened rafters of the Crow's Nest bookshop.

"What the hell is that noise?" Pirate's Cove police chief Jack Carson stared ceilingward, his blue-green eyes wide with alarm.

Ellery Page, mystery bookshop owner and Jack's boyfriend, took his oat-milk-laced coffee from Jack's unresisting hand. He said glumly, "The building is haunted."

"Since when?"

"Since the Sing the Plank organizers announced there'll be an amateur talent stage at the festival."

"*Ah.*"

They listened in silence for a moment to the muffled *twang* of a banjo and *plink* of a...ukulele?

WHOOOOO... Whoooo.... Whooooo....

"Despite evidence to the contrary, the only souls suffering the torments of the damned are yours and mine."

Jack grinned, sipped his coffee. "Is this going on during business hours?"

Ellery nearly choked on his coffee. "Don't even joke!"

"Sorry. Have either of them ever performed before an audience?"

"It seems so. Kingston and his late wife were active in their local folk music club, and Nora used to perform regularly at Pirate's Cove's Traditional Music Society."

Jack's brows rose. "I didn't know we had a Traditional Music Society."

"We don't. Not anymore. I have my suspicions."

Jack chuckled, started to speak, but was interrupted by Watson, Ellery's black spaniel-mix puppy, who dropped his squeaky toy and began to howl.

Aaah-oooooooh... Ow... Ow... Ow... Aaah-oooooooh...

Ellery sighed. "Right. That started yesterday. I'm not sure if he's protesting or auditioning." He called to the puppy, "It's okay, buddy. It's almost over."

"Speaking of almost over." Jack's tone was regretful. "I've got to get down to the station."

"Coward."

Jack shook his head, leaned across the sales counter, and kissed Ellery lightly. "I came for the drinks, not the band."

Ellery laughed.

Jack headed for the door, bending to tap Watson's upturned nose with his finger. Watson cut off his serenade mid-note, looking ever so slightly sheepish. "Working late tonight?" Jack asked Ellery.

Ellery nodded.

"Are you staying at my place or heading out to Captain's Seat?"

"Your place if that's okay."

"Best news of the day." Jack winked and went out.

The brass bell on the front door swayed, chiming a fond farewell.

It was the autumn equinox and summer was officially over.

September on Buck Island was lovely. The sun cast its lazy spell over glittering water and silky sand. The skies were blue, the breezes balmy, and the crowds had thinned.

Considerably.

Which was the not-so-good news if you were in the business of selling stuff to tourists.

The Crow's Nest clientele was not primarily of the tourist variety, but there was no denying the influx of summer visitors had plumped up their coffers significantly.

If autumn on Buck Island was anything like winter, trade was going to get pretty lean pretty fast, and Ellery was reluctantly weighing whether he did in actual fact need two full-time employees, in addition to himself, to meet the needs of their fairly slim customer base.

He was fond of both Nora and Kingston, so the idea of letting either go—and really, there was no question of who was on the chopping block—brought him zero pleasure.

"What if we carried a few book-related gift items?" Nora mused as they drank their "elevenses" coffee and gazed out at the largely empty harbor.

Nora Sweeny was Ellery's right-hand man. Er, woman. A small but stalwart seventysomething Buck Island native, she favored denim skirts and sensible shoes, and she always wore her long, silver hair in a ponytail.

"Why? We're a bookstore."

Nora shrugged. "A few extra dollars here, a few extra dollars there. It all adds up."

"If we start selling gift items, it's liable to look like we're trying to compete with some of the gift shops, which is not going to go over well."

He was thinking specifically of Janet Maples and Old Salt Stationery. Janet had only recently begun to warm up to him.

As usual, Nora understood him perfectly. "What if *our* book-related gift items were mystery-themed?"

"Hmm."

"I've been looking through that pile of catalogs in the junk room —"

"You mean *my office?*"

"Er, your office, and I've come up with a list of possibilities." She fished around in her pocket and handed over a long and crumpled list.

Ellery smoothed out the paper and squinted at Nora's cramped writing. "Cozy mystery coloring books? Murder mystery dinner party game? Cozy mystery day planner? Nancy Drew jigsaw puzzles? Mystery-themed Christmas ornaments?"

"The holidays are coming."

"You say that like it's a good thing." Nora looked at him in surprise. "I'm kidding," Ellery said, although he wasn't entirely sure about that. Last Christmas had been a total catastrophe. And just when he'd started to feel optimistic about this year's holiday season, Jack had mentioned in passing that his family really, *really* wanted him to come "home" for Christmas.

Nora said, "There are key chains, pins, earrings..."

"There's a lot to choose from," Ellery agreed. "My concern is the financial outlay."

"You have to spend money to earn money."

"You have to *have* money to spend money," Ellery retorted.

"We could start with a few choice items and see how it goes."

Ellery sighed. It wasn't that he didn't like Nora's idea. But, having only recently pulled out of the red, he was understandably cautious. Last year, he'd had his savings to fall back on. This year, he had no savings left with which to weather the inevitable inevitables.

Nora studied him. "Or not. Kingston's come up with what I think is a very good idea for bringing in new customers."

"Kingston has?" Not that Ellery didn't think Kingston was full of good ideas. He was just surprised to hear Nora touting them. Not so long ago, Nora had viewed Kingston as a rival and competitor, if not outright villain. Slowly but surely, that had changed, which was yet another reason Ellery really didn't want to have to break up the act.

Nora said—in the tone adults use to try to convince toddlers that vegetables are delicious mealtime treats, "What if we were to offer a children's story hour on weekends?"

Ellery gazed at her in alarm. "We who? We don't sell children's books. Do they even make mysteries for children?"

"They do, dearie, but we wouldn't have to limit ourselves to mysteries."

"We're a mystery bookshop."

"Yes. We are. We're also the island's only real bookstore. Which presents us with a unique opportunity to serve Pirate's Cove's smallest customer base."

"Smallest and most financially strapped."

Nora chuckled. "If there's one thing people like to spend money on, it's their children. And even more so, their grandchildren. As you've remarked once or twice, Pirate's Cove does lean toward an aging demographic."

"No offense intended."

"None taken. What Pirate's Cove *doesn't* have are endless amusements for little ones."

"These kids are the descendants of pirates. Maybe they *prefer* brawling and boozing."

Nora snorted. "While the children are listening to such classics as *Pete the Pirate* and *The Pirates Next Door*, their parents can browse our mystery-themed gifts or pick up something *they* might like to read."

"And who exactly would be conducting this story hour?" Ellery asked warily.

"Kingston."

"*Kingston?*" Ellery relaxed. "Oh. Well, in *that* case, yeah. That's not a bad idea. In fact, it's kind of a good idea. Are we going to purchase copies of these storybooks?"

"A few. I'm sure we'd sell a handful or so." Nora eyed him knowingly. "And you could probably come in an hour or so later on Saturdays. Kingston and I can easily handle the sales floor during that period. Especially during our slow season."

Ellery considered the possibility of extra weekend time with Jack, and beamed at her. "Actually, Nora, that's a *great* idea."

Nora's smile was perhaps just a tad smug. "I'll let Kingston know you've given us your seal of approval."

* * * * *

Dylan Carter, one of Ellery's closest friends in Pirate's Cove, phoned shortly after Ellery returned from lunch on the pier.

"What do you say to lunch?"

Watson, with his tendency to bark at the ever-present seagulls—as well as other dogs, babies in strollers, and every stray piece of trash the wind picked up—was not always the ideal mealtime companion, but he was Ellery's most frequent, so it was disappointing to have to turn Dylan down.

"I'd have said sure, but I already ate."

"Ah. I see." Dylan sounded more distracted than disappointed. "Well, what about joining the rest of us for dessert? Or a drink. Or both."

"The rest of us who?"

In addition to owning the neighboring Toy Chest and managing the Scallywags, Pirate's Cove's local theater guild, Dylan was also one of the organizers of Pirate's Cove's annual Sing the Plank maritime music festival, but Ellery's fear was that by *the rest of us* Dylan meant his girlfriend, September St. Simmons.

Dylan's relationship with September had grown increasingly rocky over the past couple of months, and Ellery wanted to give wide berth to any potential public uproar. He still cringed for Dylan when he recalled the most recent eruption at the Salty Dog.

But Dylan said, "Lara Fairplay and her entourage, for starters. The Sing the Plank organizers —"

"*Lara Fairplay?*" Singer-songwriter Lara Fairplay was headlining Sing the Plank, and while in his previous life Ellery had not been a huge fan of folk music—Harry Styles was more to his taste—even he was aware that getting Lara Fairplay to appear at their relatively small festival was a huge coup for the island as a whole and the organizers in particular.

"Lara, her husband, her sister...Sue." Dylan's tone seemed to grow vague.

"Wait a sec," Ellery interrupted. "Her sister Sue *or* her sister *and* Sue. As in Sue Lewis, my archnemesis."

Sue Lewis was the owner and editor in chief for the *Scuttlebutt Weekly*, Pirate's Cove's newspaper. Unfortunately, from their first meeting, Sue and Ellery had rubbed each other the wrong way—and things had gone downhill from there.

"Now, you don't really think Sue is your archnemesis," Dylan chided. "That's ancient history, isn't it?"

"*I* don't consider Sue my archnemesis, no. Emotionally mature adults don't think in such terms. *She* considers me *her* archnemesis."

Dylan squashed a sound that was probably a laugh. "She really doesn't. Her community service has changed her. She's…er…she's a kinder, gentler Sue. You'll see."

"I'll see from a distance," Ellery said. "Seriously, though, I already took my break. I can't just leave Nora and Kingston to —"

"Yes, you can!" Nora chirped from behind him.

Ellery scowled at her.

"We're fine here. Go. Have fun!" Nora made shooing motions.

"See?" Dylan put in. "Nora's got it under control."

"Yeeeah. Just a reminder to you and Nora: I'm actually the one in charge here."

From opposite ends of the island, Nora and Dylan chortled at this quaint notion.

"Okay, whatever, but I really can't just —"

Dylan cut in with an apologetic, "The thing is, I have an ulterior motive in asking you to lunch."

Ellery sighed. "Just as I suspected."

"But before you agree, you need to, well, see the lay of the land."

"*Before I agree?*" Ellery gave a disbelieving laugh. "That's taking things for granted."

"Well, after all, everyone in Pirate's Cove knows this kind of thing is like catnip for you."

"What kind of thing?"

"Mysteries. Puzzles. Games."

Ellery was not fooled by frivolous talk of games and puzzles. "You want me to solve a mystery?"

"It's a paying gig. We—well, most of us—want to *hire* you."

If anything, Ellery's caution grew. "You want to hire me to solve a mystery. What *kind* of mystery?" He couldn't help adding, "And who *doesn't* want to hire me? Sue?"

"I suppose it's a bit of a...a whodunit," Dylan said, hesitating over the first question and ignoring the second.

Uh-oh. "Who done *what*?"

Dylan said airily, "If you want to learn the answer to that—and other questions—you'll just have to come to lunch. The Seacrest Inn at one o'clock."

And with that, he hung up.

CHAPTER TWO

At the height of her fame, one well-known reviewer had referred to Lara Fairplay as "Bob Dylan without the pretty face."

That had been back in the day. The days when Fairplay had been a rising star with two crossover hits, one on the country charts and one on the pop. The days before she stabbed a woman in a bar fight. Before Lara served eleven years in prison for voluntary manslaughter.

Kind of a career killer, that last one.

Which was partly how the organizers of a rather small and obscure maritime music festival had ended up scoring such a well-known performer as their headliner.

What the infamous Ms. Fairplay thought of the Buck Island gig was anyone's guess. She sat, sphinxlike, eating her seafood salad and sipping her sparkling mineral water. She was tall and thin and very brown, as though she spent every minute in the sun. Her salt-and-pepper hair was long and curly. Her eyes were dark and surrounded by laugh lines, though she had not smiled once during lunch, so far as Ellery could tell.

He was seated directly across from her. Which meant he was also across from her husband and manager, Neilson Elon, as well as her sister and PA, Jocasta. Neilson was sleek and willowy. He wore snakeskin boots and a nearly overpowering aftershave. Jocasta was like a watered-down version of her older sister. Smaller, slighter, blonder. She wore oversized blue spectacles that Ellery surmised were more about camouflage than vision correction.

Though Lara Fairplay seemed to have forgotten his existence as soon as they were introduced, Neilson and "Jo" never took their eyes off him. He assumed they were trying to decide if the good people of Pirate's Cove were out of their ever-loving minds.

It was a question that kept Ellery up at nights, too.

Also present at the large luncheon table were Dylan (of course), Sue (unfortunately), Olive Earl, David Fish, and Philippa Jones (the three other Sing the Plank board members), and (puzzlingly) Jane Smith.

Jane was one of the Silver Sleuths book club's charter members, and Ellery was confused for several minutes as to whether Jane was there in her capacity as an amateur sleuth. That would be awkward for many reasons, not least because, frankly, Jane had as much qualification as he did to stick his nose into other people's business.

But as the conversation continued around him, he remembered that a couple of weeks earlier, Jane, who worked in one of the island's many antique shops, had discovered a scrap of music behind a drawer in a nineteenth century escritoire, or secretary desk. The music was rumored to be a half-completed song by Stephen Foster, AKA The Father of American Music, called, "Angel Beneath the Waves."

He wasn't sure why Jane seemed to be the accepted "owner" of the document in question rather than Oriel Dolin, who owned the antiques store where the scrap of music had been discovered, but no one seemed in doubt as to Jane's proprietary rights.

Anyway, Jane's discovery had sounded unlikely at the time, and it still seemed pretty unlikely to Ellery, but there

Jane sat, chatting away to David Fish about the authentication process.

"From what I understand, any historical document has to be examined from three different aspects: historical, scientific, and stylistic. I suppose, in this case, musicality will figure in somewhere, but then that's subjective, isn't it?"

"That must take some time," Fish said. "The festival kicks off Friday night."

"True." Jane directed an apologetic glance in Neilson's direction.

Neilson stopped staring at Ellery long enough to say, "So long as the appraiser is comfortable giving us a conditional thumbs-up, Lara will go ahead and perform the song on Friday." He smiled grimly. "Even if the document can't ultimately be authenticated to everyone's satisfaction, the press Lara's performance will generate is worth every penny."

If only Nora had been present to inquire how many pennies they were talking about. The trace of smugness in Jane's tiny smile led Ellery to think the Fairplay contingent was offering her a pretty decent amount, though probably not what she could get on the open market.

On the other hand, a bird in hand... Document authentication could take a fair bit of time (and money) as Ellery had learned from the mystery novels of John Dunning—with sometimes mixed results. Jane always seemed to be strapped for cash. Maybe it seemed smarter to take what she could get and let the Fairplays worry about whether the music was the real thing.

"How much of the original song is left to perform?" Fish, who owned and operated Garden Isles Florist, was also the leader of the Fish and Chippies, Buck Island's favorite home-grown folk band. His curiosity was only natural.

Jane looked vague and murmured, "Well, I'm no musician, but there's enough—"

Neilson cut in with a brusque, "Verse and chorus. That's it. Lara's completed the song herself, which is why her performance is going to be *legend*. Her first original piece since she started performing again."

"Isn't it exciting?" Jane exclaimed, gazing around the table.

Fish was noncommittal, but the rest of the committee seemed thrilled. Sue was scribbling notes like mad. Neilson smiled at Jo Fairplay. Jo Fairplay smiled at her older sister. It was a hopeful kind of smile, but Lara seemed unaware of the smile or her sister or her husband or really the entire luncheon table. She finished her sparkling water and, without a word, went outside to smoke a cigarette.

Feeling Dylan's gaze, Ellery glanced at him, and Dylan did one of those chin-over-the-shoulder moves straight out of a 1940s gangster flick.

What the what?

Ellery pushed his chair back in tandem with Dylan, and they strolled in the opposite direction of Lara, through the white French doors and onto the grassy knoll overlooking the beach below.

"So. What do you think?" Dylan kept his voice low, though they were well out of earshot of anyone but the seagulls.

Ellery said honestly, "I don't know what to think. I think Lara Fairplay doesn't want to be here. I think that's an uncomfortable family dynamic the three of them have going on. Also, I think Fish doesn't like the idea of Lara co-writing with Stephen Foster when Stephen Foster doesn't get a vote."

"Right, right. But I mean, about taking the case?"

Ellery cocked his head. Dylan was probably about sixty (he was always vague about his actual age). A short, slim, dapper man with boundless knowledge of film and theater in addition to a wide array of other interests. His eyes were blue and lively, his nose rivaled Barrymore's, and his silver hair was always cut in the latest style. He was very good at many things, but in particular, he was good at talking people into doing what they didn't want to do.

"What case? Nobody said a word about what the case is or wanting me to take it."

"We're trying to keep as much of a lid on it as we can. They wanted Sue there for publicity, but that did complicate things."

"That's Sue."

"It's just that this kind of situation can sink a festival, and it's the first year we might even get out of the red."

"Okay, well, obviously I want to help. But—"

"And of course, they had to take a look at you and…sign off, as it were. There was no point going into details if they weren't on board."

"Wait a sec."

"Lara and Neilson. Not *literally* sign off." Dylan cleared his throat. "That is, well, yes, literally, in as far as the rest of the organizers will want some kind of contract, I guess. Really, it's for your protection, in case things do go south."

Ellery's unease began to expand exponentially, much like the black plague had once crept across Europe. "South? How far south?"

Dylan said promptly, seriously, "Deep south."

"Like 'My Old Kentucky Home' south? Or—"

Dylan cleared his throat. "Further south than that."

Ellery said slowly, carefully, "Dylan, what *exactly* are we talking about?"

"Just that... Obviously, we don't want you to be held liable if something does happen to her. To Lara, I mean."

Whatever the question would eventually be, there was only one answer, and that was *no*. To be precise, *oh hell no*. And yet, that crucial combination of consonant and vowel, that single syllable safe word, was *not* what popped out of Ellery's mouth.

Instead, fatally, he heard himself ask, "Why would something happen to her?"

"From the moment her name appeared as Sing the Plank's headliner, Lara started receiving death threats."

"Death threats." Ellery's tone was flat. Been there done that.

"Yes."

Ellery glanced back at the greenhouse-style café and the more distant lighthouse where Lara Fairplay, long hair whipping in the wind like someone in a 1980s music video, stood on the edge of the green overlooking the rocks and water.

"Then Jack's the one you should have invited to this case of indigestion."

"No way. Lara won't have anything to do with the police. Believe it or not, the minute this came up, I suggested talking to Jack. It didn't go well. She's very bitter about, well, a lot of things, but her incarceration in particular."

"That can't have been fun. She did plead guilty to killing someone, though. But that's not even the point. You know I don't have the resources to deal with a situation like this. Besides, what makes you guys think whoever is threatening her would follow her to the island? It's probably some nut in Tennessee who doesn't like the idea that she's planning to resume her career. I'm surprised she doesn't get *more* crazy letters."

Dylan looked interested. "Why Tennessee?"

"Why *not* Tennessee? I'm just saying, you don't have to be in proximity to someone in order to threaten them. I used to get some very weird fan mail."

Come to think of it, he *still* got weird fan mail now and again. Special delivery. As in, dropped off at the Crow's Nest by someone on the island.

Still.

Dylan said, "You're right, which is why we're all so worried. The threats originated *here*. In Pirate's Cove."

"*Here?*" Ellery gazed at him in exasperation. "Why didn't you lead with *that*?"

Dylan opened his mouth, but his excuse was forever lost to posterity as a third party joined their cliffside tête-à-tête.

"*REALLY*, DYLAN?" a woman demanded in a tone intended to strike fear into the hearts of men.

It worked. Dylan and Ellery both jumped guiltily and turned to face September St. Simmons.

September was about twenty years Dylan's junior. She looked like a lot of actresses of a certain age: trim, toned, and toothy. She had long dark hair and false eyelashes. No doubt she had eyes as well as lashes, but those Bambi lashes were what you remembered.

"September! Darling!" Dylan exclaimed with fake heartiness. Ellery thought he lost color.

"Don't *darling* me." September stormed—quite literally (Ellery felt a drop or two of something that was probably not rain)—up to them. "Dylan, I specifically asked to be included in any get-togethers with Lara!" She spared Ellery a glance. "I should have known!"

"Huh?" Ellery said. "I'm just an innocent bystander."

"Oh, don't give me that. You're always egging him on."

"W-w-what?" It was so ridiculous that Ellery, unfortunately, laughed. Out loud.

Dylan winced. September turned a shade of scarlet that was flattering to no living creature, and turned her back on Ellery—which was some maneuver, given that it meant stepping between him and Dylan.

"This wasn't a social gathering," Dylan tried to explain. "This is an official meeting of the festival organizers."

"You're having lunch!"

"It's a committee lunch meeting. You're not on the committee, my dove."

"Neither is Jane or Sue Lewis or *him*."

Dylan threw *him*, er, Ellery, a look of apology.

"September, *darling*, Sue is handling promotion for the festival. Jane was there at the request of the Lara's manager. The presence of food doesn't make it a social occasion."

"And what about *him*? Why was *he* invited? What festival business is *he* involved in?"

"I'm just going to step inside..." Ellery began a strategic retreat, but froze as Dylan, seeming to lose all patience, suddenly shouted, *"None of your bloody, damned business, woman!"*

Even the seagulls seemed to have nothing to say in the wake of that outraged bellow. For a few startled seconds there was nothing but the crash of waves on the shore below.

September recovered quickly.

"How *dare* you talk to me like that." Her eyes blazed with fury. "When I think of everything I put up with? Sometimes, I think I could kill you, Dylan."

Dylan snapped back, "Let me tell you, darling, the feeling's mutual."

"Hey, you two," Ellery warned. "You've got an audience."

Dylan and September followed the direction of his gaze. Across the rolling width of wild green hillside, Lara Fairplay was staring at them.

CHAPTER THREE

"**D**ylan Carter just phoned," Nora announced when Ellery arrived back at the Crow's Nest. "He wants you to phone him back. Do we have the case?"

"No."

"*No?*"

Ellery, bending down to receive Watson's joyous greeting, said, "Not as far as I know. Lara went for a walk after lunch and never came back. I slipped out early."

"Oh?" Nora's brows shot up. "Did your leaving early have anything to do with Miss St. Simmons showing up unexpectedly?"

Ellery gave Watson a final pat and rose. "Sometimes I wonder whether you've got a telescope stashed in the attic. How on earth could you know that, Nora?"

A discreet cough floated from the Gothics and Ghosts section. Kingston's disembodied voice said apologetically, "I ran into Miss St. Simmons as I was returning from lunch. She was in a bit of a tizzy."

"*Tizzy?* Is that a euphemism for full-throttle tantrum? Because she was threatening Dylan's life when I left."

Ellery nearly missed Kingston's mild, "Good heavens," as Nora said briskly, "Excellent!"

"*Excellent?*"

"Yes. Perhaps now he'll give her the old heave-ho."

"The old heave-ho? You've got some interesting dating customs on this island."

Nora was not distracted by Ellery's teasing. Indeed, she had an uncharacteristically brooding look. "Drastic times call for drastic measures."

"Yee-ah. I wish you wouldn't say that kind of thing out loud."

"Men can be *such* fools. It was obvious from the start that woman was a menace. But boys will be boys. All it seems to take is a pretty smile, long legs, and big—" Nora's impatient hand gesture seemed to indicate a predilection for cantaloupe or perhaps watermelon.

"I beg to differ. We're not all of the same ilk." Though Ellery was equally unenthralled by September's...garden variety charms, this came from Kingston, who wandered out of the Gothic section, brushing off a gossamer strand of cobweb. "In my opinion, nothing is more sexy than a mature woman of intellect, sincerity, and good humor."

Nora preened as though this comment was intended as a compliment to her, and for all Ellery knew, it was.

"This is all very enlightening," he said, "but I don't want to hear any more about what you two find sexy."

Kingston and Nora chortled, but Nora was serious when she asked, "Why do you suppose Miss St. Simmons was so angry at not being invited to lunch?"

"She didn't say, but she did make it clear to Dylan that it was important to her to be included in any get-togethers with Lara Fairplay."

"Perhaps she's lonely for other showbiz people," Kingston suggested. "From what I understand, she's had trouble making friends on the island."

Dylan had never said so to Ellery, but he didn't doubt it.

"She's had coffee with Jane a few times," Nora said. "If she's had trouble fitting in, it's trouble of her own making. No, I snum she imagines there's a career opportunity to be had. Does she sing?"

"Probably," Ellery said. "Everyone else on the island seems to."

"Maybe she's simply a fan," Kingston offered.

"What's the case?" Nora inquired, apparently losing interest in the subject of September St. Simmons's social life.

"Hmm?"

"The case you're being hired for."

"I wasn't hired," Ellery reminded her. "I was being considered. I'm not sure there *is* a case, really. After Lara agreed to appear at Sing the Plank, she started to receive death threats."

Nora and Kingston exchanged looks.

"But speaking as someone who used to be in the public eye—and given her history—that might not be totally unexpected."

"If her people are contemplating hiring a private investigator, it would seem to be *fairly* unexpected."

"Just a routine reminder: I'm not a private investigator. I think maybe what made everyone uncomfortable was that these threatening letters seemed to have originated here."

Kingston studied Ellery over the tops of his spectacles. "*Here?* On the island?"

Ellery said, "Anonymous letter writing is apparently a popular pastime in Pirate's Cove."

Kingston was, unsurprisingly, confused by this comment, and Ellery wished he'd kept his mouth shut as Nora launched into an explanation of how, since moving to the village, Ellery too occasionally received anonymous hate mail. Nora and Kingston were speculating that perhaps

Ellery's poison-pen pal had branched out to include visiting musicians, when Ellery finally interrupted.

"My point is, I received weird emails before I ever moved here, and I'm sure Lara does too. They come with the territory."

Kingston looked thoughtful. "Perhaps one of the local bands isn't happy that the festival committee went off-island this year to hire a headliner."

"I'm sure *none* of the local bands are happy about that," Nora commented.

That was a surprise to Ellery. "Is that possible? Is this the first time the Sing the Plank headliner is a mainland act?"

"It's not the first, and I'm sure it won't be the last, but it's been quite a few years since someone was brought in to headline from outside. I think there are some hard feelings about that. Not least because the rumor is Ms. Fairplay is being paid significantly more than any local band. Past or present."

"Oh. Ouch. Yeah, that could breed some hard feelings. In fairness, she'll have travel and accommodation expenses local groups wouldn't. Unless the festival's covering all that too?"

"Yes. Perhaps. Of course, if she brings the crowds the organizers are hoping for, she'll be worth every penny."

"If she was drawing the kind of crowds she used to draw, I doubt if Sing the Plank's organizers could afford her," Kingston observed.

"True," Ellery said. "Plus, she'd be booked years out. But she's still bound to bring a larger crowd than the Fish and Chippies." He met Nora's frown. "Hey, I bought their CD. I bought the T-shirt. I'm a fan. But it's a fact that someone as well-known as Lara is going to be a bigger draw."

Kingston said reminiscently, "That first album of Lara's was wonderful." He hummed a few bars of "Fool Me, Fool You," and Nora joined in. They beamed at each other.

Ellery said, "Even if someone in a local band got their nose out of joint and decided to send Lara hate mail, it's still unlikely they'd act on any threat. Hopefully, it's just a way of venting their frustrations." He was thinking as much of his own poison-pen pal as Lara's.

"Hopefully." Nora's tone was not overly encouraging. "In any case, you should phone Dylan and see if you passed the audition."

"Are you in?" Dylan asked when Ellery returned his phone call a few minutes later.

"Am I?" Ellery answered cautiously. "I'm still not sure what the organizers want me to do. I'm not a PI, and I'm definitely not a bodyguard."

"Lara's road crew handles her security. But they're more like bouncers than security professionals."

"Is that similar to me being more like a bookseller than a security professional?"

Dylan argued, "You're a bookseller who's very good at finding out stuff. And you have a team of—"

"*Please* don't say professionals," Ellery pleaded.

"Professional-grade snoops for sure, which is bound to be helpful."

"Maybe. But honestly, Dylan, I think Lara—or her people—should talk to Jack. I understand her reluctance and why she might dislike law enforcement in general, but Jack's not only good at his job, he's...kind. He's a good guy. I mean, he really is. He'll try to help her, regardless of her criminal record."

"I think the world of Jack," Dylan responded. "But he hasn't figured out who's sending *you* threats yet."

"How do you— Does everyone on this island know I'm getting anonymous hate mail?"

"Not *everyone*. Sue hasn't mentioned it."

"Oh, well. I feel so much better, then. Unless Sue's the one sending them."

Dylan seemed amused at the idea. "Sue's got her faults, but poison-pen letters aren't her style."

"Nope, her style is publishing libelous insinuations in the local paper for everyone on the island to read." Ellery made the effort to let go of old grievances. "Anyway, since I haven't even managed to figure out who's sending *me* hate mail, there goes your argument."

Dylan was undeterred. "But *think*: if this is some nut looking for publicity, a police investigation is the *last* thing we want to do. That attention would just feed their psychosis. And maybe they'll escalate. We don't want this to turn into an even bigger problem. We need this year's festival to be a success. I'm not exaggerating. If we can't at least break even, this may be our last Sing the Plank."

It was a good argument, and Ellery was certainly sympathetic. He couldn't help pointing out, "But what if it's the other kind of nut? The kind of nut who really does mean to do Lara harm?"

"I've already discussed this with Lara and Neilson as well as the committee. If that's your determination, if you decide there really is a case and Lara really is in danger, then we'll hand everything over to Chief Carson, and it will be his headache."

Ellery opened his mouth, but then Dylan's words sank in. "Wait. You're saying all I have to do is figure out if the threat seems legit?"

"*Exactly!* You've had a lot of experience with this kind of thing by now. It shouldn't be hard for you to tell if this is more than some rando angry that Lara is out of prison and pursuing her career once more."

"I guess so." Ellery was still reluctant.

"And you're going to be paid. I did some arm twisting, and the committee has agreed to come up with five hundred dollars, which Neilson agreed to match. So you're going to get a thousand dollars for, basically, a weekend's work. That's not so bad. Right?"

"No. That would be pretty helpful, actually."

"So it's a win-win."

"Let's hope," Ellery said.

After agreeing to meet with Lara and Neilson that evening at Loon Landing, the site of the festival, Ellery ended the call with Dylan and phoned Jack.

He had uncomfortable experience with how fast news traveled through the village, and he didn't want to add criminal omission to the additional charges he might have already incurred in Jack's eyes.

One of the advantages of being the police chief's boyfriend was he could forgo the delights of on-hold music and public-service announcements, and just call Jack on his cell. Unless Jack was in a meeting, he always picked up by the second ring.

"Hey. What's up?" Jack's usual brisk tone was warm.

"Welllllll…"

"Uh-oh." Jack sounded resigned. "What have you got yourself into?"

"Hopefully nothing too serious." Ellery explained Lara's situation and the music festival's organizers' decision to bring in someone unofficial to snoop around.

Jack listened in silence. When Ellery finished, Jack said, "I can't say I'm thrilled."

"No. I know."

Jack's sigh was just a wee bit weary, and Ellery winced inwardly. Jack was the most conscientious person he'd ever known. He didn't enjoy knowing he was adding to Jack's worries.

Jack said, "It's a lot of responsibility. You understand that, right? You're all hoping there's nothing more serious going on here than some crank venting his or her frustrations, but that's not always the case. Without exception, the authors of these types of communication are vindictive, spiteful personalities with little to no self-control."

"Right. I realize this person's not normal."

"That's correct. You're very often dealing with mild to moderate paranoiacs, manipulative personalities suffering from grandiose delusions and other antisocial character disorders, or those with more serious mental illnesses."

"That's the part that worries me," Ellery admitted.

"You have reason to be worried." Jack was not much for sugarcoating.

"They're only here for the weekend, though."

"If this stalker really is locally based, that's *maybe* good news."

"They have to be local, don't you think?"

"It's probable. Assuming the threats really did originate here. Do you know for a fact someone checked for postmarks?"

"According to Dylan, yes. The envelopes were postmarked here in Pirate's Cove."

"Then this person is either local or working with someone local. Local or within traveling distance."

Ellery would, of course, have preferred the threats to originate long-distance. He was mostly reassuring himself when he said, "I've been getting threats since May, but so far, luckily, that's all it's amounted to. Hate mail. Maybe that's all it is here. Maybe the person is working out their antisocial tendencies through the postal service."

There was a decided lack of reassurance in Jack's grim, "Sometimes the harasser loses interest in the game. Sometimes they find another target."

"Exactly. So—"

"Sometimes they escalate."

Neither spoke for a moment. Ellery shook off his unease.

"The tentative agreement I made with the festival organizers and Lara's manager is that if I decide the threat is real, Lara Fairplay will come to you."

Jack said, "Again, that's a lot of responsibility. You're not a psychologist. You're not a profiler."

Ellery's sigh was at least half groan. "I *know*. Believe me. I don't know why it's so hard for me to say no."

Jack made a soft sound of exasperation. "I do. Ell, I'll help you—unofficially—however I can, but I really wish you hadn't involved yourself in this."

Me too.

"Thanks, Jack. I mean it." Ellery added in afterthought, "You're taking this a lot better than I expected."

"Am I?" Jack's tone was bland. "Maybe it turns out we have two actors in the family."

Ellery chuckled, relieved that Jack seemed more resigned than exasperated, and then Jack told him he had to get back to work.

It was a couple of hours later before Ellery registered the fact that Jack seemed to think they were maybe part of the same family.

CHAPTER FOUR

Lara Fairplay was singing.

> *Bravest of angels, return thee to me,*
> *From under the waves and over the sea,*
> *Gone is my peace, my heart aches with woe*
> *The dearest of men lies sleeping below.*

"Huh." Ellery, uncomfortably folded into one of the vintage chairs in the somewhat musty Loon Landing Boathouse Theater, was noncommittal as he listened to what was starting to feel like the world's longest sound check.

He was not familiar with the works of Stephen Foster. He was barely familiar with the works of Lara Fairplay. And while he could appreciate the cultural significance—not to mention the social-media currency—of Fairplay performing a long-lost work by Foster, he had kinda expected, well, something else. Something more original. More exciting.

"Of course, it must be an earlier work," Jane, sitting on his left in the mostly empty row of chairs, responded to what she must have perceived as criticism. "Maybe even a discarded effort."

"It's only the one verse and chorus, right?"

"Yes. Lara wrote the rest of the song herself."

"Did she write the music too?"

"She must have. There was only a scrap of lead sheet with a few lyrics."

Ellery nodded thoughtfully. He could feel Jane watching him in the gloom.

"So the appraisal went okay this afternoon?"

Jane smiled. "Did you think it wouldn't?"

"I didn't know. I wasn't sure if the testing could be completed in a few hours."

"Oh, they've yet to do the forensic testing of ink and paper. But that can take quite a long time. And no one wanted to wait."

"I guess not." Why did he have the odd feeling that Jane was laughing at him?

Onstage, Lara made a broad thumb-across-her-throat gesture, and the band—two rhythm guitars, fiddle, and drum kit—broke off with a couple of trailing and discordant notes.

Another discussion with the sound engineer ensued. This was interrupted by Neilson Elon, who appeared onstage to debate the lighting.

Jane leaned over to whisper, "Do the Silver Sleuths have a theory yet as to who might have mailed those threatening letters?"

Aware that there had been a falling out among the Silver Sleuths following Jane's discovery of the Foster fragment in her place of work, Ellery offered a neutral, "Probably. But I've yet to hear it."

In the dim light he saw Jane's mouth curve in a sour smile. "If I were you, I'd take a good, hard look at Jocasta."

"Lara's kid sister? Really?" Ellery automatically scanned the rows of empty seats for Jo Fairplay. He spotted her hunched over in the front row, busily typing notes into an iPad.

"Yes."

"But the letters came from someone in Pirate's Cove."

Jane said, "Lara used to spend summers here when she was young. Which means, so did Jocasta. She could very well still have friends on the island."

"I didn't know that."

"Nora's not the only one with her ear to the ground. You also might not know that Jocasta was trying for a career in music, too. She didn't get anywhere until Lara went to prison. But once Lara got out, Jocasta made the decision to return to working as Lara's PA. Except, I don't think it was *entirely* her choice."

Ellery turned to study her. Jane smiled another of those humorless smiles. "People don't talk to me like they do you. They do something even more useful. They forget I'm in the room."

Having zero idea how to respond to that slightly unsettling statement, Ellery resorted to a neutral, "Ah."

"Of course, I'm not a mental-health expert, but I do believe those three have a very interesting emotional ménage à trois."

"I'm not sure I know what that means."

Jane tittered. "Ménage à trois? It's French for—"

"No, I know what the term means. I'm not sure what *you* mean."

"You must have seen the movie *All About Eve*? Well, this is the musical."

"But didn't you just meet them all today?"

Jane preened. "I had a private dinner with them last night. It was *very* enlightening."

"I bet. That must have been fun."

"Yes. It's nice to be appreciated by talented, successful people who don't enjoy looking for the worst in others."

Ellery nodded noncommittally.

That was a slap at the Silver Sleuths. From the first, Jane's former comrades had been openly skeptical of her find, which, understandably, she'd not taken well.

Perhaps because of their occasional—well, let's be real, MORE than occasional—peripheral involvement in some of the island's high-profile investigations, the members of the Silver Sleuths book club had developed a certain skepticism toward their fellow man, much akin to that of a jaded big city detective nearing a well-earned retirement. Plus, Jane had lived on the island for little more than a decade, which still made her an outsider in the eyes of many. Maybe that factored in, too?

Whatever their reasoning, Jane was, not surprisingly, hurt as well as angry at the suspicion directed her way.

After all, life *was* full of lucky coincidences and timely happenstance. Ellery could testify to that. The problem was, he *also* was dubious of her claim.

It seemed too convenient that Jane should stumble across such a find at the very moment when a prospective buyer, who might be willing to take some shortcuts in the verification process, should appear. Such things did happen, but did they happen to the Jane Smiths of the world?

He asked cautiously, "Are you going to be at the book club on Tuesday?"

"No. Nora made it clear I was no longer welcome."

"Did she?" He didn't think Nora would be deliberately unkind, but she could be painfully blunt. Sometimes that New England forthrightness could feel like sandpaper on an open wound. And perhaps Jane had reason to be sensitive.

He pulled a page from his mother's playbook and said, "Maybe certain people, whose names we won't mention, have their noses *a bit* out of joint."

Jane brightened. "I think so, too!"

"You have to admit, it's an amazing thing to have happened to anyone."

Jane's eyes glittered with warring emotions. "But it *is* the kind of thing that happens to *someone*."

So why not Jane Smith?

"True."

"If it was going to happen to anyone, it would probably be someone who owned or worked in an antiques store."

"That makes sense," Ellery agreed. "I guess part of the... concern is that Buck Island was so far out of Stephen Foster's world. Er, his milieu? That's what I've heard. How could his desk end up on this island?"

"Oh, the desk wasn't *his*," Jane said quickly. "Or at least, it needn't have been his. We don't really know the provenance of the desk, only that it belonged to one of the island's wealthy families. It could have traveled from anywhere to the island. The desk itself is genuine, but who knows beyond that?"

"Right. Right." He asked sympathetically, "Will you have to share the proceeds from the sale of the music with Oriel Dolin?"

A look of caution flickered across Jane's face. "I'm going to give her something, of course, but the desk was actually mine. I'd purchased it a week earlier."

"I see."

This was a new piece of information, and it did nothing to allay his doubts. That nineteenth century escritoire would doubtlessly be an expensive piece of furniture. All the items in Oriel Dolin's shop were frighteningly expensive. Some legitimately so. And Jane was frugal in the extreme. The likelihood of her purchasing a very expensive and certainly unnecessary piece of furniture was, well, *unlikely*. And that that particular piece of furniture should then be discovered to contain a hidden, valuable item? That was one heck of a lot of coincidences.

He was jolted out of his thoughts as Dylan flung himself into the velvet-covered chair on his right. The chair squeaked ominously, and Dylan, Ellery, and Jane all sneezed in the cloud of dust that pouffed out of the aged upholstery.

"What do you think?" Dylan demanded.

Ellery returned, "About...?"

"Anything. Everything."

"No one has said a word to me about anything. Let alone everything."

"*I* said something to you!" Jane objected.

Dylan said, "Oh, hello, Jane. I didn't see you there."

"Right." Ellery said. "I mean, I haven't been able to speak to Lara or Neilson yet. I'm hoping I can have a word after the sound check."

Dylan read between the lines. "I'm not sure what's going on," he admitted. "Yesterday... Neilson was pushing hard for the committee to take some kind of action to ensure Lara's safety, but when I tried to speak to him earlier this evening, he seemed annoyed I brought it up."

"Maybe they've changed their minds about how serious the threats are."

"It's not *they*. Lara's in a world of her own. I'm not sure she knows or cares threats have been made."

They fell silent as Neilson began to argue with one of the festival's volunteer lighting techs.

"Great. The crew is already ready to mutiny," Dylan muttered. "It's not bloomin' Carnegie Hall."

No, it sure wasn't. Most of the people involved in putting together Sing the Plank were volunteers. Less than half of the sound technicians were part of Lara's own road crew, and Lara's people were about the only personnel being paid for their time.

After a minute or two, Lara interrupted Neilson's discussion, and though their conversation was too far from the mics to be picked up, her impatience came through loud and clear.

As did Neilson's defensiveness. They went back and forth, and then Neilson put his hands out as though to say, *I'm just trying to help!*

Lara turned her back, gave a hard, decisive strum of her guitar, and the first chord of her biggest hit, "Fool Me, Fool You," shot through the dark theater like an arrow released from the bow of a master archer. She took a long stride toward to the mic stand, and the band came in as her head tilted to the mic.

"*I could spot your con a million different ways...*"

It was as if someone threw all the doors and windows open. Music washed over the sea of chairs, flooding through the theater like a sudden gust of clean, cold air. Everyone seemed to take a deep breath and relax.

"That's what I'm talking about." Dylan slid down in his seat, as though settling in.

He wasn't the only one. Lara was on solid ground as she belted out the song with all the energy and confidence of an actual performance.

"*I know how the cards play out...*"

Ellery's gaze wandered. He saw Neilson join Jocasta in the first row, and didn't think he imagined the look of melting sympathy Jo threw her brother-in-law.

He observed them for a moment before turning his attention back to the stage. He had not been inside the theater before, but he'd heard a lot about it.

The Loon Landing Boathouse Theater had begun life in the 1800s as a working boathouse on the estate of Quinton Jones. The boathouse had sheltered Jones's pride and joy, a motorboat named *The Merlin*, until the boat and Jones were lost off the coast in a summer storm.

By the 1960s, the Joneses' family fortunes had fallen, and their seventy-five-acre estate had begun to be sold off in parcels. The pretty cove with its private landing and boathouse had been one of the last pieces of land to go. It had been acquired by a Hollywood movie producer who'd planned to turn the dilapidated structure into a movie revival house. Renovations had been more than halfway complete when the producer had gone bankrupt and been forced to sell off the theater along with his summer home.

Finally, in the 1980s, Loon Landing had been acquired by Pirate's Cove's city council for the annual maritime music festival as well as other island events. That original festival had lasted a short five years and then fizzled out, only to be reborn a decade later when Dylan had arrived on the island full of enthusiasm and energy and plans to turn the island into the theatrical capital of the Eastern Seaboard.

Well, no. But Dylan had definitely wanted to nurture and grow the island's small performing-arts community. Which he had done very successfully.

As for the boathouse, there had been renovations through the years—that incredible floor-to-ceiling window with its view of the ocean which formed the backdrop for the performers, was the most notable—but the theater was not in terrific shape. The stage, in particular, was not in terrific shape. After a close call the previous autumn, the old trapdoor had been nailed shut to prevent any unplanned exits from the limelight.

It was going to cost a pretty penny to make the renovations necessary to bring the structure up to current building codes, so Ellery could understand Dylan's worry that another year in the red was liable to be the end for more than just the festival.

As someone valiantly struggling to save his own beautiful historic albatross, Ellery could sympathize.

It would be a shame to lose all that history—not to mention one of the few pieces of real estate on the island preserved as public resources for the residents' recreation and education.

"You must be excited, Jane." Dylan leaned past Ellery. "Hearing that scrap of music brought to life?"

Jane's eyes lit. "Oh yes. I can't tell you how satisfying it is."

"Have you heard the whole song yet?"

She shook her head regretfully. "I'm going to have to wait till tomorrow night like everyone else."

The three of them jumped in unison as a blood-curdling scream ripped through the theater, cutting off Lara's performance. The band played a couple of horror-stricken chords before stopping.

"What the—" Dylan began.

Jocasta was on her feet, pointing up at the scaffolding, as one of the PAR can lights suddenly dropped. Everyone began to shout.

The room itself seemed to suck in a sharp collective breath as the light hurtled down toward the stage where Lara stood.

Lara, clutching her guitar to her as if it were her child, leaped aside a split second before the light smashed into the wooden planks.

Jocasta burst into tears. Neilson rushed up the steps and onto the stage. He grabbed Lara.

"Oh my *God*." Dylan was out of his seat, making his way to the stage. Ellery followed on his heels.

"I'm fine, I'm okay," Lara was responding to the chorus of questions and concern as Dylan and Ellery reached the apron of the stage. She looked pale, but her voice was steady. "It missed me completely."

"I *told* you we needed to take these threats seriously!" Neilson was saying.

Lara glared. "*I told you so?* Really? That's your contribution?"

"Because I *did* tell you so!"

She planted her hand in his chest, pushing past him and walking to the edge of the stage. "*Jo!* For God's sake. Pull yourself together. You're not helping."

Jocasta nodded, still sniffling, and wiped her eyes on the sleeve of her *The Byrds* sweatshirt.

Ellery vaulted onto the stage as Neilson turned on Dylan. "You said she'd be safe performing here!"

Well. *That* cat was out of the bag. Ellery studied the smashed light. Like everything else in the theater, it had been somewhat the worse for wear even before it fell forty-five feet to its crash landing.

Dylan ignored Neilson, speaking intently to a stricken-looking Fish before turning back to Lara and her husband-manager.

"The festival committee said from the beginning that we couldn't make any guarantees. The whole point of bringing

Ellery in was to see where we were with this...this unique situation."

Ellery put his hand on Dylan's arm. "Shouldn't we check the scaffolding to see whether this was an accident? It's an old theater. Accidents happen."

Dylan looked startled. Fish looked relieved.

"He's right!" Fish said. "The building's practically falling down."

Dylan threw him a look of exasperation.

"*Oh, terrific,*" Neilson exclaimed. "We've been booked to appear in a deathtrap!"

"Nonsense," Dylan protested. "This theater is perfectly safe. It's weathered over a century of storms and...and... safety inspections."

"No, he's right." That was Lara, and she was looking at Ellery. "It *is* an old building." She added to Neilson, "Come on, Neil. We've played worse venues."

"Not since the early days."

She lifted a dismissing shoulder. "Everything old is new again."

"It's not a song, Lara! If that thing had hit you..."

She smiled sardonically. "You'd collect all that lovely insurance money."

Neilson's head went back as though she'd slapped him.

"*Lara,*" Jocasta protested. "You don't have to always take it out on Neil! He's only trying to protect you."

"Don't worry, I'm used to it, Jo," Neilson said bitterly.

Lara gazed ceilingward as though asking for strength— or maybe a bolt of lightning she could use.

Dylan and Ellery exchanged looks. Ellery raised his brows meaningfully, and Dylan called, "Stage manager, can we get one of the crew to take a look at this light?"

CHAPTER FIVE

Watson was howling when Elliot arrived at Jack's around ten that evening.

He wondered uneasily how often Watson treated Jack's neighbors to his songs of protest. Watson was a people person—well, a people pup—and all the chew toys and soft blankets in the world couldn't compensate for finding himself alone.

Ellery unlocked the front door. "Hey. What's all this?" Watson hurled himself cannonball style into Ellery's arms. "It was just a couple of hours!"

Watson proceeded to detail his complaints—the list was long—and Ellery took a couple of minutes to soothe his four-footed pal's injured feelings.

"If you want to go back to having a puppysitter, we can do that." It was convenient being able to drop Watson off at Jack's, but Ellery didn't want to put Jack's neighbors in the position of having to complain to the chief of police about his boyfriend's air-raid siren—er, dog.

When Watson was done venting, Ellery went into the kitchen to make a hot drink. Jack usually had a beer when he got home. Ellery was too wound up to sleep, but he didn't want more alcohol. He found the herbal tea he'd left in Jack's cupboard and brewed a cup. He did not leave many items at Jack's: a toothbrush, a couple of books, and the box of passionflower tea were about it. Though he was spending more time at Jack's, he still wasn't completely comfortable on Jack's turf. It wasn't anything Jack did or didn't do. Jack kept a carton of oat milk on hand for Ellery and randomly bought packages of prewashed salad mix. In case Ellery got the sudden urge to graze? Jack expected—wanted—Ellery to feel at home. But Jack's pristine domicile was a slightly intimidating reminder of how completely and utterly self-contained Jack was—and how long he'd been so.

Granted, Ellery only felt that way when he was alone in Jack's house. When Jack was there, the place felt entirely different.

He was drinking his tea and trying to make sense of the evening's events, Watson curled on the sofa beside him, when Jack's key scraped in the lock.

Jack opened the door, and the weariness in his face lightened at the sight of Ellery. Watson took the opportunity to once more express his feelings on various topics of public interest.

"Get a lawyer," Jack told him, and proceeded to kiss Ellery hello.

"Long time no see," Ellery said eventually.

"It does feel like it." Jack kissed him again, lightly. "How was *your* day?"

"The day was routine. The evening was a little weird."

"Yeah? Step into my office and tell me about it."

They adjourned to the kitchen. Jack poured himself a beer and picked up Watson for a cuddle. Ellery had another cup of tea, smiling, as he watched Jack avoid Watson's best efforts to also kiss him hello.

When Jack's light gaze caught Ellery's, his smile seemed to warm Ellery's entire chest.

"So what are the Silver Snoops up to now?"

"Believe it or not, this is not Silver Sleuths related. Except maybe tangentially." Ellery related the dramatic turn the night had taken.

"How the hell was this not called in?" Jack was frowning as he set Watson down.

"Because the crew's consensus was, it was an accident."

"*An accident?*"

"Accidents do happen."

Jack studied Ellery thoughtfully. "But *you* don't think it was an accident?"

"I don't know."

Jack considered this, smiled faintly. "You must have a theory."

"It's...pretty crazy."

"Your batting average isn't so bad. Let's hear your theory."

"I'm starting to wonder if this whole death-threat thing could be a publicity stunt."

"*Ah.*"

Ellery met Jack's keen gaze, his own expression wry. "It's not that I have any reason to think so. Nobody said or did anything that made me think they aren't taking these threats seriously." He mentally replayed that and amended, "Well, it's hard to know what Lara believes, but the others seem to be taking the threats seriously."

"So?"

"So I'm just thinking it's got to be daunting for Lara to try to climb her way back to the top after that kind of fall from grace. It's more than losing momentum. The entire music business has changed. Everything's changed. And the industry is notoriously tough on older performers."

"It's not like she's starting from scratch, though."

"No. But in some ways that might be easier. Now it won't just be about her music anymore. It's going to be about *her*, her past and whether, in some people's view, she has a future. She's never going to be mentioned without her prison record getting dragged into the conversation."

"I don't know that's true. Look at Vanessa Rayburn. Look at Elizabeth Perry."

Jack was that rarity: a cop who read mystery novels. That said, most of his mystery reading had been done back when his favorite authors were Franklin W. Dixon, Robert Arthur Jr., and Donald J. Sobol.

"Okay. That's fair," Ellery conceded. "Even so, comparison is tough on the ego. And Lara seems like someone who doesn't cut herself or anyone else any slack."

Jack thought it over. "Maybe."

"She's invited me to have breakfast with her at the inn tomorrow, so maybe I'll have a better feeling for the situation after we talk."

Jack took a swig from his beer bottle. "You're the theater expert. How likely is it that lighting equipment could fall accidentally?"

"I mean, a lot is going to depend on the knowledge and diligence of the run crew. The festival crew are volunteers and mostly amateurs. Lara's got her own skeleton crew and presumably they're more experienced, but lighting is always one of the most dangerous things happening onstage. In addition to the risk of electrocution, there's the risk of fire. There's the risk of falling over cables and wires. Plus, lights are really heavy. They're secured to rigs and scaffolding with tethers and safety cables. If something isn't properly battened down, it isn't just the lights that can fall. The whole support beams and rigging can come crashing down, and it can happen fast."

Jack mulled that over. "You've got a lot of people working backstage, I assume?"

"Yes. Working. Waiting. Rehearsing."

"How easy would it be to sabotage the lighting equipment?"

"Stage crew would have the best chance of getting away with it. Once a performance starts, anyone who doesn't belong backstage is going to stand out like a sore thumb."

"But, as you've pointed out, you've got two teams working backstage that don't really know each other."

Ellery said, "That's true. I think it would have to be someone comfortable with being backstage, though. Most non-theater people get lost backstage. Especially in the dark."

"Okay."

"The thing is, it's not like anything was cut or broken. It looked like a cable was improperly rigged, and then snagged on a batten, which snagged on some drapery. A lot of the festival equipment is old. The sound system. The lighting equipment. It's all seen better days. The boathouse itself is...well, I'm sure you've seen it. Honestly, anywhere else and I think that stage would be condemned."

"Then it could have been an accident."

Ellery said, "It absolutely could have been an accident. It probably *was* an accident. It's just that the timing feels a bit coincidental."

"I agree. I'll do some checking around tomorrow."

Ellery let out a breath he hadn't known he was holding. "Thanks. That would be a relief."

Jack's expression was quizzical. "Having second thoughts about taking this case, Mr. Brown?"

Mr. Brown was a reference to the boy detective Encyclopedia Brown books, which Jack had read back in the days of Little League and lunch boxes.

"Second, third, and fourth. When I saw that light fall..."

"Mm." There was a wealth of experience—and understanding—in that monosyllable.

"How was *your* day?" Ellery asked as Jack finished his beer. He put his teacup in the sink. His own day had been long, and he was more than happy to bring the curtain down on it.

"Same old, same old. There's a lot more politicking involved in being police chief than I ever imagined."

Ellery tipped his head. "Do you regret taking the job?"

"No." Jack spoke without hesitation. "They needed someone from the outside. I think I've made changes that make policing easier and the island safer. There's always a trade-off."

That was the truth.

Ellery smiled. "Speaking for myself, I'm glad you took the job."

Jack grinned, and pitched his beer bottle with unerring accuracy into the kitchen recycle bin. "You're definitely one of the perks, Mr. Page."

A short time later, as they were undressing in the small, tidy bedroom, Jack said, "Howard struck a plea bargain."

"Did he?" Ellery draped his shirt over the back of the vintage valet stand he'd found at Captain's Seat and had repaired and refinished for Jack as a thank-you-for-everything. A gesture which Jack had seemed disarmingly surprised and even touched by.

"Yep."

Ellery opened his mouth to ask, but Jack said dryly, "He still insists he acted alone."

"Maybe he did."

"Maybe."

"Either way," Ellery said, "chivalry is not dead."

Jack snorted. "Is that what you call it?"

"Chivalry in the first degree?" Ellery made an inquiring face.

"Yeesh."

Ellery grinned at that un-Jack-like utterance. "I have news too. According to the island underground, Cyrus has a new lawyer." He folded his jeans and dropped them on the seat of the valet. Jack was not typically one for ripping one's clothes off and scattering them around the bedroom—though he had his moments.

"Good luck with that. It's going to take more than another lawyer to get him out of the jam he's in."

"Mm."

"Mm?"

"It occurs to me, it's going to get increasingly awkward as people I've helped put in jail get out on bail or get parole or serve their time and come back to Pirate's Cove." Ellery was partly kidding, although the fact that he'd felt it necessary to speak at Ned Shandy's bail hearing had brought home the risks of amateur sleuthing in your own backyard.

"Welcome to my world," Jack said wryly.

"Oh. Right. I guess that *is* a problem. Especially in a village." Ellery took a moment to privately admire the sight of Jack's lean, tanned body in nothing but white T-shirt and white stretch boxer briefs. He definitely preferred the scenery at Jack's bungalow. "I guess a lot of people hold grudges?"

Jack pulled back the quilt and bedclothes and climbed into bed, avoiding dislodging Watson, who was already snoozing comfortably at the foot of the bed. "Some people do, for sure. Some people take responsibility for their actions. Some people take their arrest and prosecution personally. You get used to it." He glanced at Ellery and amended, "*I'm* used to it. I don't know how you'll deal with it."

"Maybe I won't have to deal with it."

Jack said mildly, "If you're planning to live in Pirate's Cove for a significant amount of time, you're eventually going to run into someone who blames you for poking your nose into their business. Unless you're planning to give up sleuthing?"

Ellery brooded over that unlikelihood for a moment or two. "Have you ever had to arrest a friend?"

Jack gave him a funny look. "Not so far. I came closer than I liked once."

Ellery realized which particular *once* Jack was referring to. He said, "I can't pretend that didn't hurt."

"I know. But you don't go into law enforcement if you're afraid of conflict."

"Probably not." Speaking as the guy who once upon a time had done almost anything to avoid conflict—especially if it meant hurting someone else.

Later, after Jack had spent some time silently but efficiently making up for past transgressions, he murmured, "You know my family's been trying to get me to fly to LA for the holidays."

Ellery had been drifting in a pleasantly dreamy bubble of contentment. The bubble popped. But he'd known this was coming. He drew in a breath, said with determined good cheer, "They miss you. You haven't been back in how long? It's understandable."

"I miss them too." Jack also drew in a breath as though bracing himself. "But I don't want to go back this year."

"You don't?"

"No." Jack gave him a sideways look. "It's your first Christmas on the island. I want to be here."

Just like the Grinch, Ellery felt his heart grow three sizes bigger. "It would be nice to have you here," he admitted.

Jack nuzzled him beneath his ear. "Yeah?"

Ellery hunched his shoulders, laughing. "Yeah..."

"You're very ticklish."

Ellery laughed again, but to his surprise, Jack backed off.

"However."

"However?"

"There's a catch."

"What catch?"

"They're coming here."

"Who?" Ellery remembered what they had been talking about a few seconds earlier. His eyes popped open. *"Your family? Here?"*

Jack sounded amused. "Not into the bedroom, no. Although...they have to sleep somewhere."

Ellery opened his mouth but was forestalled by Jack's, "My parents aren't like yours. If I suggested a hotel, there would be words."

"Gotcha. But that's okay. I'm looking forward to meeting them."

Jack made a noncommittal noise.

Ellery thought he understood. "Jack, if you're not ready to introduce me to your family as your boyfriend, that's okay. I get it. We haven't been seeing each other that long, and it might send the—"

"If you're about to finish that sentence with *wrong message, we're* going to have words," Jack interrupted.

"Which words? So long as the words aren't *we're breaking up*—"

"Hell no, we're not breaking up. Nor am I worried about sending the wrong message because there's only one message: I care very much for you, and...and that's it."

Hopefully the expression on his face was not as goofy with happiness as he felt. "Okay. Well. I mean, I feel the same, obviously. I'm happy to meet your family or *not* meet your family. Whatever you want."

Jack's long sigh sounded a lot like one of Watson's moans.

Despite his confusion, Ellery had to bite back a laugh. "Jack."

"Listen." Jack's expression was earnest, his green-blue eyes soft with uncharacteristic emotion. "I *want* you to meet my family. I want them to know you, and I want you to know them."

"Well, then..."

"But."

"But?"

"I don't want you hurt by someone saying something stupid."

Ellery blinked. *Ohhkaay.* He hadn't seen that one coming. He asked cautiously, "Does your family not realize you're gay?"

Actually, Jack was probably bisexual, but in this case, it was kind of the same difference. What didn't make sense, given what he knew of Jack, was that Jack's family wouldn't know his sexual orientation.

"They've known since I was in high school." Jack's smile was wry. "Did you ever see that movie *Guess Who's Coming to Dinner*?"

"Of course. It's a classic."

"Well, there's a lot of truth in that film. My family had no problem with friends and colleagues being gay, but when *I* came out, they struggled. Which is to say, they thought maybe I was mistaken."

Ellery considered and discarded several responses. He settled on a neutral, "Hm."

"When I fell in love with Hannah, they latched on to the idea that I'd worked out the kinks."

Ellery cleared his throat.

Jack added, "In a manner of speaking." He brooded for a moment. "Their current position is that I'm still not over everything that happened with Hannah and the baby."

"*Ah.*" And who could say they were completely wrong. Did you ever really, completely get over that kind of tragedy?

Jack offered a weary, apologetic smile. "They mean well, but…"

"The road to hell is paved with good intentions?"

"Yeah. They wouldn't deliberately be hurtful, but they could hurt you all the same."

Ellery studied Jack's troubled face. He smiled with what he hoped was reassurance. "Forewarned is forearmed. And you know, I'm not going to crumple up and die because someone says something thoughtless. Have you ever seen my reviews for the *Happy Halloween* films?"

"Er, no."

"*Brutal,*" Ellery assured him cheerfully. "So long as *we're* on the same page, I can handle your family's…doubts."

Jack closed his eyes as though Ellery was the one who'd said something hurtful, but then his lashes lifted and he rested his hand against Ellery's cheek. "I'm very lucky to have you in my life. Don't think I don't know that."

"It wasn't luck," Ellery said. "It was persistence, determination, patience, your beautiful blue-green-green-blue eyes, and the fact that you like my dog."

Jack laughed. "I do like your dog." He reached for the lamp switch. "And I do like you."

CHAPTER SIX

"I bet you're sorry you let Carter talk you into this gig." Lara Fairplay smiled faintly as she drizzled honey into her tea.

"I'm happy to help," Ellery replied. "But honestly, if someone really is stalking you, you should go to the police."

They were having breakfast in Lara's sunny suite at the Seacrest Inn. It was just the two of them. No sign of Neilson or Jocasta, which made Ellery hopeful he might finally something useful. This Lara, barefoot with a thin, pink, silk dressing gown thrown over jeans and T-shirt, seemed quite different from the Lara of the previous day. More open? Less guarded maybe? Or maybe she'd just finally had a good night's sleep. The sound of the waves at night was pretty soothing.

Lara said, "I'd rather die than ask the police for help." She took a bite of jam-slathered English muffin, adding, "No offense."

"No offense?"

"I know you're tight with the police chief."

"He's a good friend, but that would be my advice anyway. I'm not a professional investigator or anything like that. Whereas Jack—our chief of police—has a ton of experience. He was a homicide cop in L.A. before he moved to the island. Plus, he's a really nice guy. He's got a good heart."

She said gently, "When I say no, I mean no."

Ellery considered her for a moment, then nodded. "Okay. Well, I tried."

"Yep. On my head be it."

"I guess then we should start with the obvious question. Who do you think is sending these threats? Could it have to do with performing the Stephen Foster song?"

Lara's lips parted. "You know, that never occurred to me. I guess anything's possible. There are probably people out there who resent the idea that I'd have the audacity to complete Foster's work. There are people who don't think his music should be played at all." She shrugged. "Is it possible? I guess so. I don't think it's likely."

"Then what do you think is going on?"

Lara meditatively crunched her muffin. She swallowed finally, and said, "First, you have to understand that I get a lot of weird and threatening email. Even before Dawn Shumway. It's the nature of the business. People I barely know, heck, people I've never met, ask for favors. Ask?" She gave a short laugh. "Try *demand*. Or they blame me because their own music career didn't pan out. It's white noise. You get used to it. What makes this different—potentially different—is that these letters came from Pirate's Cove. And I do know—well, used to know—a couple of people in Pirate's Cove who might still be holding a grudge. It seems like they'd have outgrown all that by now, but maybe not."

"Who?"

"Arti Rathbone and James Sutherland. Assuming they even still live on the island. They might not."

The Rathbone name was familiar, but James Sutherland rang no bells.

"What would Sutherland and Rathbone have against you?"

Lara's smile was pained. "My family used to spend summers here when I was growing up. We came every year, and I made friends. I was in my first band here. We called ourselves Backsplash Butterfly."

"Yikes," said Ellery.

Lara chuckled. "Right? But honestly, we weren't so bad. As a matter of fact, we were pretty decent. Anyway, every summer I'd come back and we'd gig around the island. Eventually, we got the idea we'd try to shop a demo of a song Arti and I wrote."

"What was the song?"

"'Eyes to Heaven.' It was...not bad for total beginners; let's put it that way. Nothing happened with the song, but the label, White Wine Records, offered me a contract."

"You. Not the band?"

"Me."

"Okay. I see." Ellery did indeed see. "And you accepted their offer?"

"Of course I did. Who wouldn't? But Arti and James felt I'd betrayed them. Which was illogical. I couldn't *make* the record company take them. They knew I planned on having a career in music. It wasn't like we'd always dreamed of doing that together as a band. *They* were the band. I was a featured artist during the summers. That's all."

"Did they make threats?"

She made a face. "Not like *we're going to kill you.* More like, *karma's a bitch* or *we hope we're there when you get yours.* Ill-wishing more than actual threats. We were kids. Emotions always ran high. I felt bad the friendship was over, but I never took the threats seriously. I still don't. It's been more than twenty years. But Neilson thinks they could be behind the letters."

"And you agree?"

"It would be ridiculous to still be hanging on to that kind of grievance. But I can't think of anyone else in Pirate's Cove who would have it in for me."

"Did you keep the letters?"

"No."

"*Why?*"

Lara's brows rose at Ellery's tone. "Because I never keep that stuff. It's just negative energy. It's not like we're going to take it to the FBI. When the letters kept coming, maybe we should have hung on to them..." She finished vaguely, "Neil thought they might upset me."

"It was your husband's decision not to keep the letters?"

Lara regarded him for a moment. She gave a cynical smile. "That's right. You run a mystery bookshop. Don't worry. My husband isn't trying to knock me off."

"That's what they all say," Ellery told her. He wasn't totally kidding.

She laughed. "Probably. But the problem for Neil is, I changed my will *and* redid my insurance policy when I was in prison. If something happens to me, everything goes to Jocasta. Which brings up the second problem for Neil—and Jocasta. I was worth a lot more *before* I went to prison."

"I didn't know you could get life insurance in prison." Ellery was momentarily distracted.

"You can if you're an A-lister. Once upon a time, I was an A-lister." There was no self-pity. It was a statement of fact.

"Okay. Well, do your husband and sister know about these changes?"

"Yes." Lara's smile didn't reach her eyes.

"Did your sister also spend summers on the island?"

"Of course."

"She had friends of her own in Pirate's Cove?"

"Not really."

"No?"

Lara hesitated. "Jo has always been defiantly introverted."

"That's an interesting way to put it."

"Isn't it?" Lara said, "If you're thinking Jo is writing these letters and then sending them to someone in Pirate's Cove to mail them for her, no."

"Why not?"

"It's not her style. Anyway, she's more of a dreamer than a doer."

"Is it true that your sister is also trying to launch a music career?"

Lara didn't roll her eyes, but the effect was the same. "Like I said, Jo's a dreamer, not a doer."

Whoa. Ellery hoped his expression didn't reveal what he was thinking. He'd always wanted siblings when he was growing up, but with a sister like Lara, who needed natural enemies?

Or maybe Lara was just keeping it real. Maybe eleven years in prison knocked all the sugarcoating and sentiment out of you.

"Did you keep in touch with Sutherland and Rathbone?"

"I tried. I hoped we'd eventually get past it. We were close. I cared about them." She shook her head. "But no. They weren't having any of it. Like I said, I have no idea if they're even still on the island. Neither planned on staying here past college."

Ellery thought over what he'd learned. "Okay. Well, it gives me a place to start."

"Does it? It all seems pretty unlikely to me."

"Then you don't think the threats are real?"

Lara seemed to mull it over. "I don't know." She gave an odd smile. "I'll tell you something. After the last eleven years, *none* of this feels real."

No kidding. He felt his first flash of sympathy for her.

"If the threats aren't real, what do you think is going on?"

Lara contemplated him for a moment. "Good question."

* * * * *

When Ellery arrived back to the Crow's Nest after his breakfast with Lara, he fully expected to hear Nora and Kingston haunting—er, rehearsing for Sunday's debut. Instead, he discovered nearly the full contingent of the Silver Sleuths in assembly.

"I'm not saying it *couldn't* happen." Nora's voice carried clearly as Ellery knelt to unfasten Watson's harness. "I'm only saying it's *highly* unlikely."

"Here we go again," Ellery whispered. Watson, eyes shining, tongue lolling, wagged his tail.

Hermione Nelson retorted, "But isn't that true of all these discoveries? Who was that American school teacher who found that lost sonnet by Shelley in an antiques shop in the Lake District?"

"Grace something?" Mrs. Ferris offered.

"She *worked* in an antiques shop," Nora said. "She didn't find the sonnet there. She found it...well, somewhere else. Which is my point."

"What is your point?" Ellery inquired.

The Silver Sleuths—having missed the sound of the doorbell because, as usual, they were all talking at the same time—greeted him with more guilt than delight.

"Oh, *there* you are, dearie!" Nora exclaimed.

"And here *you* all are," Ellery replied.

Kingston, who had snatched up a stack of books for reshelving, offered an apologetic smile and headed post-haste for the Thriller and Suspense section.

Hermione, a stout woman in her late 60s with piercing blue eyes and alarmingly red hair, was not so easily cowed. "Stanley couldn't make it. He's unwell," she informed Ellery.

"I'm sorry to hear it. I hope it's nothing serious."

"Personally, I suspect he's afraid of crossing swords with Jane Smith."

Ellery, who had reached the register and was in the process of counting cash, stopped to stare at the ring of watchful faces on the other side of the sales desk. "I don't think he has to worry. Jane told me she's, er, resigned her commission."

This elicited gasps all around.

Hermione said, "I expected this."

"What does *that* tell you?" exclaimed Mrs. Ferris.

Mrs. Ferris was an on-again-off-again member of the Silver Sleuths. She was a small, wiry woman with curly gray hair and dark eyes. She was fond of cats, gardening, and true crime. She had seen every single episode of *Dateline* and had a not-so-secret crush on Keith Morrison.

"I know what it tells me," Ellery said. "She doesn't feel welcome anymore."

This was met by a rare and disconcerting silence.

"I'm not sure I understand why any of you would be crossing swords with Jane Smith? Especially here of all places."

"Because she's a fraud, dear." Edna Clarence, a tall and stately blonde, was probably around the same age as Hermione, though she'd have no doubt denied it. She had only lived on the island a mere thirty years, not nearly as long as the other book club members.

"What do you mean, she's a fraud? Since when?"

"Since forever, I imagine," Nora said briskly. "I've always been skeptical of her origin story."

"Her...origin story? I thought you were all pals. Partners in crime-solving."

Hermione put in, "First she was married, then she wasn't married. Which *is* it? She could never seem to say."

"Huh?"

Kingston, having shelved that stack of books in record time, returned to the desk. "Jane's alleged discovery of a hitherto unknown work by Stephen Foster continues to raise doubts."

"It passed the initial appraisal."

"Says who?" Hermione demanded.

Which was a good point. What kind of professional standing did this document appraiser really have?

Nora seemed to read his mind. "Where did the Fairplay people find someone willing to authenticate such a potentially valuable document at a moment's notice? Did Jane recommend this person? Perhaps the scam is more far reaching than we imagine."

"I see." Only too well. Maybe it was inevitable that their suspicions regarding the Foster fragment would lead to more widespread skepticism about Jane's bona fides. At the same time, Jane hardly seemed like a master criminal.

He said, "Would she really take that kind of chance, though? Eventually, there's going to be all kinds of testing done on the paper and ink and even the content of the document. It's not like she could get away with something like that for long."

"People do. People have," Nora said.

"Okay, but in order to pull off that kind of hoax, wouldn't Jane have to have experience committing forgery?"

"Who says she doesn't?" Edna inquired.

"I agree. It's very hard to believe," Hermione said. "Jane always seemed far too timid a personality to attempt anything of a criminal nature."

Nora's sniff spoke volumes—and the entire library consisted of crime fiction.

"She could have a partner," Kingston suggested. "She could be someone's dupe."

"Now *that*, I can believe," Hermione said.

Nora said, "You *all* underestimate her."

"Okay, well, what's your theory, Nora?" Ellery asked.

"I don't have a theory," Nora admitted, which was surprising. Rarely did Nora not have a theory or six. "It's possible Jane did discover that scrap of music exactly as she described, but is it *plausible*?"

The others murmured agreement.

"I don't like the timing. It's too great of a coincidence."

"What's too great a coincidence?" Ellery pressed her. "That someone like Jane would discover the document?"

"No. Well, yes. But not entirely. That a valuable piece of folk music should be discovered in a tiny hamlet just weeks before a folk music concert takes place where one of the performers could very much use a special something to get the media's attention."

"You think Jane's discovery was tailored to Lara Fair-play's appearance at Sing the Plank? Or do you think Lara and her people are in on the scam?"

Nora beamed at Ellery. "That's *very* good, dearie!"

Ellery deadpanned, "I learned from the best."

"I think both scenarios are a possibility," Nora returned to business.

"The problem is, this is all suspicion and speculation. We don't have any proof," Ellery said. "And I get the impression, if we did have proof, it wouldn't be all that welcome."

"Ahhh," Hermione said.

"Ohhh," Edna said.

Kingston said, "Then you *do* believe Lara Fairplay and her people are in on the hoax."

"I can't guess as to what Lara knows or doesn't know, because she seems to operate on a different plane. As far as her manager and entourage, I think that even if they aren't in on the scam—assuming there is a scam—they wouldn't want to know the truth. They've already invested a lot in this enormous PR effort. I don't just mean money. I get the feeling a lot of their hopes for Lara's comeback are riding on this."

Mrs. Ferris said, "You don't think they would listen if we went to them with our suspicions?"

Ellery said firmly, "We'd have to have a lot more than suspicions before I'd be comfortable going that route. Like I said, the document passed the initial appraisal."

They weren't happy with that reminder, but it was the truth.

Kingston mused, "I wonder why she'd take such an enormous risk."

No question who *she* was.

"I think she'd do it for the attention," Edna said.

But the others shot that idea down at once. "No," Hermione said. "She avoids the limelight."

"I agree. She'd do it for the money," Nora said. "She's not well off."

Ellery tried not to think of the remorseless appraisal his own uneven finances must receive from his fellow sleuths.

"Speaking of finances," he said. "We're open for business now."

This drew blank looks all around.

He said with exasperation, "So perhaps this briefing can wait until lunchtime?"

"*Oh,*" Kingston snapped to attention. "Yes. Of course!"

"Is it that time?" Nora looked surprised. "We didn't get any practice in."

This was directed to Kingston, who considered, and then offered a tentative, "Perhaps, if you don't already have plans, we could work in a short session after dinner?"

"*Oh.*" Nora's cheeks pinked ever so slightly. "That's...I believe that might work."

Hermione and Edna exchanged glances but restricted their comments to cheery farewells, which they made as they hastened toward the front door.

Mrs. Ferris, perhaps out of pity, purchased a copy of *The Mormon Murders: A True Story of Greed, Forgery, Deceit and Death* by Steven Naifeh and Gregory White Smith.

As Ellery rang Mrs. Ferris's purchase up, she said to Nora, "It seems that it's finally over between that charming Mr. Carter and That Awful Woman."

"*Oh?*" Ellery, Nora, and Kington chorused.

Ellery winced, but there was no use pretending he wasn't just as curious as Nora and Kingston.

"What have you heard?" Nora demanded.

"It's not what I heard," Mrs. Ferris said. "It's what I *saw.* Mr. Ferris and I were having supper at the Salty Dog last night when the festival people came in after finishing setting up for the big concert."

"Right," Ellery said. Dylan had invited him to go to the Salty Dog, but he'd wanted to get over to Jack's.

"*Well,*" Mrs. Ferris continued, "That Awful Woman had been sitting at the bar all evening badmouthing Mr. Carter. No one really paid much attention to her. It just sounded like sour grapes."

"What was she complaining about?" Ellery asked.

"She was claiming Mr. Carter kept trying to interfere in her career. That he was very controlling."

"*Dylan?*" Ellery interrupted. He couldn't think of anyone less controlling than Dylan.

Nora cut in, "Interfering in her career how?"

"It wasn't clear. But I gathered it had something to do with the festival. Apparently, she *sings.*"

"*Ah,*" Nora said.

"How was Dylan controlling her?" Ellery asked.

Mrs. Ferris shook her head. "She didn't go into specifics, but the implication was she was trying to break it off and he wouldn't let her end it."

"That's *ridiculous,*" Ellery said, though his word of choice was not nearly so polite.

"That doesn't sound like Mr. Carter," Nora agreed. "Quite the opposite."

Nora and Mrs. Ferris exchanged knowing looks.

"Agreed," Mrs. Ferris said. "*Enywhoo,* she'd had quite a snootful by the time they arrived, and she went charging right up to Mr. Carter and gave him and everyone else an earful."

"Good heavens," Kingston exclaimed.

"But Mr. Carter said, just as cool as could be, *September, go home. You're drunk. Worse, you're boring.*"

"Gulp," said Ellery.

Mrs. Ferris's eyes gleamed with uncharitable glee. "And she *lost it*. The *mouth* on that creature!"

"What was the upshot?" Nora inquired.

"She told Mr. Carter it was all over."

Kingston murmured, "I should hope."

"And Mr. Carter said, *It certainly is. If you come near me again, I'm filing a restraining order.*"

"*Dylan* said he'd file a restraining order?"

"Yes. And I think he was serious," Mrs. Ferris said. "And she thought so too because she stormed out of the pub without another word."

"Well, that's that," Nora said briskly. "There's nothing to keep her in Pirate's Cove now."

"I hope so, dear," Mrs. Ferris said. "But I can't help feeling we haven't heard the last of her."

CHAPTER SEVEN

It was a slow morning at the Crow's Nest, and when Ellery asked whether Nora and Kingston minded if he took off for an hour or so to see if he could catch David Fish at the festival grounds, they assured him everything was under control.

Then again, they'd have said the same thing if the building was on fire. In Nora's opinion, sleuthing always came first. Sometimes Ellery suspected she viewed the bookshop as nothing more than a loss leader for their (only in her imagination) PI business.

Anyway, he buckled Watson into his little red harness, snapped on his leash, and set off for the festival site.

Friday was turning out to be another temperate and beautiful day. The morning sunshine bathed the entire island in luminous light. The sand glittered, every wave seemed to sparkle, and the sky was so intensely blue, it seemed to have invented a new color.

Watson made a point of barking hello to everyone he knew—as well as barking hello to everyone he didn't. Ellery paused for a word with Imelda, the receptionist at Vincent Veterinary Hospital, waved from a distance to Jocasta Fairplay, who seemed in a desperate hurry to get into the Brewhouse for coffee, and willingly went along with September

St. Simmons's pretense that she didn't see him, when they passed on opposite sides of Main Street.

When he reached Loon Landing, the cove was buzzing with activity. Volunteers struggled with the wind as they put up tents for food vendors and entertainers like Madam Buckley, the medium (who would probably take issue with the idea that she was an "entertainer"). Smaller stages were being assembled for the acts not taking part in the Boathouse concerts.

He found David Fish at the Amateur Stage in conference over the audio system with a couple of the sound men.

Fish was a nice-looking guy, probably in his forties. Tall, lanky, with merry brown eyes, long dark hair and a Van Dyke beard that suited him very well, especially when Buccaneer's Days rolled around.

When the sound system issues had been worked out, Ellery approached Fish, reintroduced himself, and asked if he could have a word.

"Sure, I know you. You're the mystery guy." Fish squatted down to give Watson a pat, and Watson gave Fish his seal of approval, delivered by tongue.

"I run the Crow's Nest mystery bookshop," Ellery agreed.

Fish rose, his grin quizzical. "It's more than that, or Dylan wouldn't have volunteered you to find out who's harassing our opening act."

"I have a knack for being in the wrong place at the wrong time."

"You do show up in the *Scuttlebutt Weekly* a lot."

Ellery winced. "Don't remind me."

They were briefly interrupted by a festival volunteer with a concern over the number of mic stands allocated for Stage 3. Fish promised to come up with two more mic stands and redirected his attention to Ellery.

"So what can I do for you, Ellery?"

"Well, to be honest, I wondered if I could get your thoughts on the whole situation with Lara Fairplay."

"*My* thoughts?"

"I'm betting you know the island's music scene better than anyone else."

Fish said, "I wouldn't say that."

"Okay. Can you point me in the direction of whom you think I *should* to talk to?"

Fish frowned, considered Ellery for a moment, then shrugged. "No. I guess not. But if your question is who do *I* think sent those threats to Lara Fairplay? No clue."

"Are a lot of the other bands upset about bringing in Lara to headline?"

Fish gave a small, irritable sigh. "Yes and no. First off, it's not like we've got that many working musicians on the island, let alone playing in bands doing traditional music. There are a handful of us, so ninety percent of the bands you're going to hear this weekend are coming in from the mainland. That's a given with any music festival."

"Okay."

"Secondly, the headliner is usually from out of town. It's just that our festival is so small, we've gotten used to the headliner being *semi*-local. Like for the last two years, we had Pat Pendragon from Narragansett. A lot of us know and have played with Pat at other festivals."

"So is it Lara's history that rubs people the wrong way?"

Fish gave a short laugh. "Talk about leading the witness!"

"Sorry. I'm just trying to get a feel for the social dynamics."

"Part of the problem is that Lara's being paid more than any headliner we've ever had."

"I can see that would cause trouble."

"In fairness to her, she's the biggest act we've ever booked. If she was still at the top of the charts, we couldn't have come close to affording her. It's only because her career's in free fall that she took the gig."

"That, and she has connections to the island, right?"

"Yeah. I guess so. But it was a long time ago, and she doesn't strike me as the sentimental type."

Ellery said, "Honestly, I have no idea what type she is. She's hard to read."

"Truth, brother."

"How did word get out about how much Lara was being offered to play?"

Fish's dark eyes flickered. He hesitated a fraction of a second before saying, "Not sure."

That seemed like a weird thing to lie about. But it did seem like Fish was, at best, hedging. Until that moment, Ellery had felt that Fish was being candid and trying to be helpful. Now he wasn't so sure.

Although maybe Fish, who was the festival's entertainment coordinator, was where the information leak had sprung. If so, it was understandable why he'd want to gloss over that slip of the lip.

"When I talked to Lara this morning, she said that threats come with the territory. She was skeptical of anyone local really posing a danger, but she did say there might be a couple of people she knew as a kid who might still have lingering hard feelings."

"Did she?" Fish asked absently, gazing out across the field dotted with colorful tents. Beyond the meadow was the salt marsh, and beyond the salt marsh was Loon Lake.

"People who might still dislike her enough to send a couple of anonymous emails, with no intention of literally doing her harm."

Fish swiveled his gaze back to Ellery. "She gave you names?"

"James Sutherland and Arti Rathbone. I guess the three of them were in a band together when she spent summers here as a kid."

"Yeah? Hm."

Ellery didn't think he was imagining Fish's abruptly distant affect. "Have you lived on the island your entire life?"

"Me? No. It'll be nineteen years next month. I grew up in Washington County."

"Right. So you don't know of either Sutherland or Rathbone?"

Fish seemed to come to a decision. His gaze met Ellery's. "I've no idea about James Sutherland. I never heard of him. Arti Rathbone is my accordion player."

Fish's band, the Fish and Chippies, had acquired a new accordion player over the summer; a slim, dark-haired woman with a Madonna-like air and musical chops to rival James Fearnley. Ellery had never known the woman's name because he didn't know any of the band's names, with the exception of Fish.

"Arti Rathbone's a woman?"

"That she is. Artemisia Rathbone. As a matter of fact, she's a direct descendant of the original Ann Rathbone."

Probably not a direct descendant, since the original Ann Rathbone had been in her teens when she drowned herself in the sea, but descended from the same bloodline, for sure. The interconnectedness of all things barely began to describe how intertwined the original families of Buck Island were.

"For some reason, I thought your accordion player was a recent transplant."

"She moved away from the island after college, but she came back after her sister passed away. She's raising her nieces and nephews in the old family home."

"That's—I had no idea. She's a really talented musician. She adds a lot to the group."

"I think so."

My accordion player? Yep, he wasn't wrong in thinking Fish wasn't keen on giving up Arti Rathbone's details. That was okay. Now that Ellery knew whom he was looking for, he didn't need Fish's help. And maybe Fish knew that too because he said reluctantly, "She has a day job at the Cloaked Owl."

"Really? Okay, then."

The Cloaked Owl was the island's only commercial provider of items used in witchcraft. Along with the bells, books, and candles, the daughters of the Cloaked Owl sold "proprietary blends of anointing and magickal oils, loose incense, and custom spells."

"I can tell you this much," Fish said. "No way is Arti wasting her energy mailing anonymous hate mail. She's not that kind of person."

Ellery said, "I believe you. But I literally have no leads. Maybe she can give me some ideas about who to talk to."

"She was away from the island for almost twenty years. I don't know what help you think she could be."

"I don't know either," Ellery said peaceably. While good accordion players did not litter the island's shores, Fish's defensiveness had to be more than that. Now that Ellery thought back, he'd had the impression that Arti's joining the band had initially ruffled a few feathers, though all the players seemed to get along fine these days.

"Thanks for your help." He scooped Watson out from under the stage, where he'd discovered an enticing hot-dog wrapper, nodded goodbye to Fish, and headed back to the village proper.

Unfortunately, the Cloaked Owl was not yet open for business. According to the sign on the door, their hours were from noon to midnight.

"Double, double toil and trouble," Ellery said.

Watson concurred with a tail wag.

"We'll try again after lunch."

He returned to the Crow's Nest, which, despite a ferry full of visitors arriving for the festival, was dishearteningly empty of anything resembling customers. Nora and Kingston stood at the counter, having coffee and debating the merits of Stephen Foster's musical legacy.

"You can't deny some of his repertoire is inherently offensive, given its historical context and racially insensitive language," Nora was saying.

"There's no question Foster benefitted enormously from the racial hierarchy of his day. But there's also no question he was writing for minstrelsy at a period when blackface performers were largely sympathetic to the plight of slaves."

"Do you think they talk like this all the time?" Ellery whispered to Watson. His work-hours conversations with Jack typically consisted of asking how each other's day was going and figuring out if they'd be able to have dinner together.

Watson had no opinion beyond tugging to be free of his halter so he could say hello properly.

Kingston said, "An argument could be made that—"

"Nora, have you ever heard of Artemisia Rathbone?" Ellery interrupted. And it clearly was an interruption. Nora and Kingston were so involved in their conversation, they didn't register his appearance until he was right in front of them.

"I've certainly heard of the Rathbone family," Nora replied, not in the least discomposed.

"*Ah*, the legend of Skull House." Kingston rubbed his hands together as though preparing to sit down at his typewriter.

"Right. This would be one of Ann Rathbone's descendants."

Nora frowned, considering. "That might be the eldest daughter. The one who ran away."

"I don't know about running away. She didn't return to the island after college."

"Same thing." Nora caught Ellery's eye and winked.

"Ha. Anyway, it seems her sister died, and so she's back here raising her sister's kids. She works at the Cloaked Owl. Oh, and she's the accordion player in the Fish and Chippies."

"I had no idea!" Nora sounded slightly aggrieved at this failure to communicate on the part of the island's most reliable gossips.

Kingston said, "One of the island's oldest families, the Rathbones."

"I'm beginning to realize that doesn't mean much," Ellery said.

For some reason Nora and Kingston seemed to find that funny, but Ellery wasn't kidding. From his perspective, the island's gene pool remained largely, even peculiarly, undisturbed after centuries of close contact with the mainland.

"What about someone named James Sutherland?"

"Sutherland..." Nora repeated thoughtfully. "That name sounds familiar. I wonder..."

"What do you wonder?"

"It was a long time ago."

"Tell me something I *don't* know."

"If this is the young man I'm thinking of, I seem to recall he committed suicide after breaking up with his girlfriend." She sighed. "Young people are so emotional."

"That'll be the one." Ellery had no doubts. After a year of sleuthing, he could spot the layout from miles away. "How long ago do you think this was?"

Nora shook her head. "More than twenty years ago. I do remember that the family moved away after the tragedy. They weren't…"

"From around these parts?" suggested Ellery.

"Exactly. They had only been on the island a decade or so. It's not as though they had roots to the community."

"Riiiight." Ellery considered. "Okay. That gives me a starting point. I'm going to see what I can find out online."

"There's always the *Scuttlebutt Weekly*'s archives," Nora called as Ellery, Watson on his heels, headed for his office. Nora was referring to the newspaper's morgue. So far Sue, for reasons known only to herself, had resisted digitizing back issues of the paper.

"No, there isn't," Ellery called back.

He sat down at his desk, briefly checked his email, then clicked onto the internet. He typed in *James Sutherland*, and in 3.44 seconds learned there were over 39,400,000 results to scroll through.

"Argh," he said, or words to that effect.

The landline phone rang at the front desk. A moment later, Nora called, "It's for you, dearie. It's Mr. Honeycutt."

Mr. Honeycutt was the lawyer handling Brandon Abbott's estate. He rarely called with good news. Ellery prepared himself for more excuses and delays, and picked up.

"Ellery speaking," he said crisply.

"Mr. Page!" Mr. Honeycutt greeted him with uncharacteristic good cheer. "How does fifty thousand dollars sound to you?"

CHAPTER EIGHT

"**F**ifty thousand dollars," Jack repeated.

"Yep."

"Fifty *thousand* dollars?"

Ellery and Jack were grabbing a quick and early dinner at the Salty Dog before heading over to Loon Landing and the evening's festivities. PICO PD was providing most of the festival security and Ellery would be attending in his role of...well, what would you call it? Professional nosey parker?

"It's crazy, right? I never thought I'd see any kind of pay-out from Brandon's estate. Mr. Honeycutt was vague on the details. I think it's film residuals or something? Anyway, there's supposed to be a check heading my way before the end of the month."

"That is...wow." Jack gave a small shake of his head and held his beer mug up. He smiled broadly. "Congratulations."

Ellery clinked his cocktail glass against Jack's mug. "Unfortunately, more than half of it's going to go to the roof. I spent the afternoon pricing what it would cost to re-place that thing, and *ouch*."

No lie. It had been more than a smidge discouraging to realize how much of his windfall would be eaten up by ad-dressing merely the most pressing house repairs.

Jack said, "I can't tell you how relieved I am to hear you say that. I have nightmares about that roof falling in on you."

That was probably not even an exaggeration. Jack was the kind of guy who really did worry about holes in roofs and the lack of security systems and cars breaking down on lonely stretches of highway. Which, admittedly, was not such a bad quality in a boyfriend.

Still, Ellery felt bound to object, "It's not *that* bad."

Jack grunted.

"But it'll be a relief to have it repaired before the winter. The roof and the electrical system. Those are the top priority."

"If by electrical *system*, you mean ungrounded circuits, wiring with deteriorated or missing insulation, circuits controlled by old-fashioned fuses rather than modern circuit breakers—"

"*Starting* to feel a little overwhelmed here," Ellery interjected.

Jack grimaced. "Sorry. I know. And you don't have to tackle everything at once. Just the life-threatening stuff."

Ellery laughed. "*Anyway.*"

"Anyway. Are you coming back to my place tonight?"

"If that's okay."

"You know, you don't have to ask." Jack was suddenly serious.

"Actually, *you* asked," Ellery pointed out.

"Right. But the point is, you're always welcome. I like..." Jack didn't finish the thought, so maybe, hopefully, the list of things he liked was too long to spell out?

"Thank you," Ellery said. "I just don't want to take things for granted."

Jack's smile was quizzical. "It's okay to take some things for granted."

Ellery's heart warmed. Before he could respond, Jack's radio crackled into life.

"Chief?" Officer Martin called into the void. "Are you there? Are you out there anywhere?"

Jack looked heavenward. "It's tempting to answer *no*."

Ellery grinned. "I'm pretty sure the earth would fly right off its axis."

"It might be worth the risk." Jack spoke into his radio. "Carson. 10-4."

Martin's aggrieved voice replied, "I'm still over at Loon Landing. I haven't had dinner yet and no one's showing up to relieve me."

Ellery smothered a laugh at Jack's expression.

"Officer Martin, are you flipping kidding me?" Jack barked out.

A cautious silence crackled across the airwaves.

"No, sir," Martin said finally.

Jack gazed at Ellery as though words failed him. He spoke into his radio. "You remember we have protocol, right? And radio codes? *And Dispatch*?"

"Right," Martin said. "But there's nothing happening. And I haven't had anything to eat since breakfast."

Jack drew in a very long breath, held it for a second or two, and then said very mildly, "You're at a festival, Martin. Grab a cotton candy."

"Okay, but—"

Jack interrupted, "En route. ETA..." He glanced at his watch. "18:30 hours." He put the radio down, stared at Ellery, who was trying very hard to look suitably grave.

"He's been working as a police officer for three years. Sometimes I think this is all an act. That they're all getting a kick out watching him yank my chain."

Ellery laughed.

Jack shook his head, but there was a gleam of amusement in his eyes. "Sure, you think it's funny now. Wait till he radios in at four-thirty to say he hasn't had breakfast." He sighed, "I better go before he follows up with a statewide emergency bulletin. Did you want a ride over to Loon Landing?"

"I think I'll drop Watson off at your place and then walk over."

Jack nodded and rose, reaching for his wallet.

"My turn to pay." Ellery rose as well.

Jack smiled. "Thank you for dinner. I'll see you later. Oh, and congratulations again."

They kissed lightly, quickly, always conscious of the crowd around them—not much missed the collective eye of Pirate's Cove's denizens—and then Jack was gone and Ellery headed to the bar to settle their bill.

* * * * *

The sun-dappled day had faded to a cool and hazy blue twilight as Ellery left Jack's beach cottage in the heart of Pirate's Cove and drove back to the Crow's Nest. He left his VW parked behind the bookshop and walked along the cobbled streets toward the Loon Landing. This was one of his favorite times of day. The air grew soft and sweet with the scent of seaside golden rod and dusty miller. Even the sound of the tide gentled, grew musical.

Or maybe that actually *was* music.

Even at a distance, the cove was aglow with lights. Music floated on the breeze between the crash and hiss of waves hitting the seawall.

All afternoon Ellery had been riding the high of his unexpected financial windfall. The realization that he could finally afford to hire professionals to do some of the most labor-intensive work at Captain's Seat was almost too much to comprehend. He'd grown used to the idea that he was always going to be scrimping and saving in order to afford only the most crucial repairs. The idea of an actual renovation made him almost giddy.

If he budgeted carefully and negotiated ruthlessly—two things he was a lot better at than when he'd arrived on the island six months earlier—he might even manage to get the second floor into reasonable shape for guests. He could invite some of his old friends for a weekend. That would be nice. While he didn't miss his old life, he did miss some of the people in it.

But as the cobblestones gave way to the old highway that had once led to the other side of the harbor, the beat of the tide took on a melancholy rhythm. The cries of the sea gulls winging their way to the rooftops and high spaces for the night sounded forlorn. He remembered that this financial windfall was an inheritance, and that his good fortune was entirely due to Brandon's untimely death.

He had not mourned Brandon's passing. Partly because at the time, Brandon's death had left him in real legal and personal jeopardy; there hadn't been time. No time to grieve the passing of someone he'd once cared for. No time even to analyze his feelings for Brandon which, at best, had been complicated.

But now?

Now he felt unexpected sadness. Sadness that he and Brandon had never met for one last drink, sadness they hadn't been able to talk things out, sadness they hadn't been able to part as friends. He was also confused by Brandon's... gift. After they'd broken up, Brandon had never made any attempt to contact Ellery, so to find himself in Brandon's will, Brandon's *sole* heir, was baffling. Why had Brandon done that? Had it been some weird way of continuing to exert control over Ellery? Had it been a kind of apology for some of the things that occurred when they were living together? Or had Brandon left everything to Ellery as a means of punishing others who might rightfully have expected to be remembered in his will?

Who knew with Brandon? It could have been all of the above.

Or maybe Brandon had remembered Ellery in his will because on some level, he still cared a little, still valued what they'd once had?

It would be nice to think that because Ellery's relationship with Brandon, though problematic on many levels, had been his first real adult relationship, and as such, had had a big impact on him. Had, whether he liked it or not, influenced the relationships that followed, maybe even his relationship with Jack in as far as he was determined not to repeat any of the mistakes he'd made with Brandon (or even Todd).

Like not being honest about what he wanted and needed, not speaking up when he was hurt or angry. In fairness, everything was easier with Jack because Jack was straightforward and direct. Jack did not let problems fester. He also didn't have any hang-ups about saying he was sorry when he believed he'd been wrong.

And if he didn't believe he'd been wrong? He had no trouble sharing that, too. But not in a way that left you feeling belittled and dismissed.

So maybe this inheritance was Brandon's way of saying sorry—Ellery preferred to think that rather than the idea Brandon was still trying to control and influence him. The thing was, Ellery would have liked a chance to have said sorry, too. Because he *was* sorry about a few things. Sorry that he hadn't tried harder to understand what Brandon was going through. Sorry that his response to being hurt had been to completely shut down and close Brandon out.

He and Brandon would never have been a compatibility match on any love quiz in this universe or the next, but Ellery was sorry he hadn't tried to be a better friend.

The Loon Landing Boathouse was alive with light and music by the time Ellery reached the festival grounds, so maybe that explained the absence of crowds wandering through the booths and smaller stages? Maybe everyone was inside the boathouse listening to the concerts on the main stage?

The haunting voice of a woman seemed to float across the marshes and grassy fields, drowning out the outside acts and entertainment.

> *I will not say goodbye*
> *Sea may rise*
> *Sky may fall*
> *My love will never die*

That would be the female vocalist of the Fish and Chippies taking a whack at the Claire Wyndham song. Lara and her band would not perform until later in the evening.

This was the perfect opportunity to lurk backstage and see what there was to see. Ellery could keep an eye on Lara and her entourage when they showed up, which presumably would be fairly soon, and he could try to talk to Arti Rathbone when the Fish and Chippies finished playing.

He cut across the grass field, passing a small booth where "Cap" Elijah Murphy was putting on what appeared to be an old-fashioned puppet show. There seemed to be an awful lot of swords and screaming in that particular theatrical production. The audience of mostly-preschoolers looked pretty alarmed.

Next door was a booth with the sign SLOSHBUCKLERS WANTED where the parents of the terrorized tots appeared to be consoling themselves with obscenely overpriced paper cups of "grog" and "rhum."

There was no sign of Jack or Officer Martin, but he did spot Madam Buckley, the medium, commiserating with Sandy Morita, who was running the face painting booth. Sadly, it seemed no visitors were interested in having their fortunes told or their features realigned.

It didn't look like this year's Sing the Plank was going to pull the festival out of the red. Not so far, anyway, but after all, it was only Friday night. Presumably the weekend would see bigger crowds.

In fact, when Ellery reached the entrance of the boathouse, it was clear that there was indeed a bigger crowd— taking up every seat in the theater.

"Sorry, the entire evening is sold out," Greta Handel informed him apologetically. Greta owned the island's only gourmet grocery store. By the look of things, she'd had the foresight not to drag her wares to the fairground, instead pitching in to handle concert ticket sales.

"The entire evening?"

Greta nodded. "It's packed inside." She couldn't help beaming.

"That's great!"

"It really is. Maybe bringing in Lara Fairplay wasn't such a waste of money after all."

"Is that what people are saying?"

"They won't be saying it now."

Ellery nodded, glancing around the busy foyer. "Is Dylan around?"

"Um… I haven't seen him for a while." Greta picked up a walkie talkie from the table. "I can radio him?"

Ellery opened his mouth, but was forestalled by someone calling, "Ellery!"

He glanced around and there was Dylan, headed his way. His expression was hard to read, but did not appear to be that of someone who had helped organize an unexpectedly successful event.

"Hey," Ellery greeted him. "I was just—"

"I need to talk to you." Dylan's hand gripped Ellery's arm in a viselike grip. "Let's step outside."

"Sure." Ellery threw Greta a quick look—she looked as taken aback as no doubt he did—as Dylan towed him toward the door.

"I'm sorry to ask, but I need a huge, *huge* favor," Dylan was saying as they stepped out into the chilly marsh-scented evening.

"Okay. Of course. What's wrong?"

Something was clearly wrong. Dylan continued to grip Ellery's arm as though hanging on for dear life. He was flushed and agitated. His blue eyes looked dark and stormy with emotion.

"September just left me a message saying that if I cared anything at all for her, I'd come to her cottage at once."

With his free hand, Dylan held up his cell phone for Ellery to listen. Ellery dipped his head. He could hear that the voice was September—he thought so anyway—but her words were garbled.

"Is she whispering?"

"I think so. I had to listen three times to understand what she was saying. Do you think someone's there with her? She sounds strange."

Ellery drew back. "*Does* she?"

"Doesn't she?"

"Honestly, Dylan, I can't make out more than a couple of words. She's asking for you to come over there, for sure. But—"

"I can't leave," Dylan said quickly. "Not in the middle of the concert. But even if I could, I wouldn't. It's over between us. I told her that. Repeatedly. But if she *is* in-in some kind of crisis, I can't just ignore it."

"Yeah, but—"

"Please, *please,* Ellery. I know it's not fair to get you involved, but you're my closest friend. You're the only person I can trust with this."

Ellery stared in alarm. "But Dylan, if I show up instead of you, she's not going to be okay with it. September dislikes me. A lot."

"She only dislikes you because you dislike her."

"I don't dislike her. I—"

"Of course you do," Dylan interrupted again. "She's *extremely* unlikeable. She's the most unlikeable woman I've ever known. And I've known *a lot* of women."

"If she's so unlikeable, why'd you get involved with her?"

"I didn't know she was unlikeable when we met! I thought she was delightful. Warm and-and..."

"Willing?" Ellery supplied dryly.

"Yes! *Of course.* And easy-going and open and supportive. But she's not any of those things. She's...pretty awful, to be perfectly honest, and I wish I'd never gotten involved with her."

"Then why the hell are you sending me over there? She's just going to take it all out on *me*."

Dylan's eyes seemed to grow darker, even haunted. "What if she's planning to kill herself?"

"*What*? Why would she?"

"She's threatened it before when she wasn't getting her way. What if she's relying on me showing up to save her? And then I don't show up!"

"But me showing up isn't you showing up."

"It's me calling her bluff. But also making sure that if she's *not* bluffing, she doesn't ruin both our lives by doing something incredibly stupid. I'm sorry to ask it of you. Believe me, I know this is beyond the pale—"

"All right. All right!" Ellery cut him off. "I'll go."

"Will you?" Dylan seemed surprised.

Ellery sighed. "Yes."

"*Thank you.* Truly." Dylan seemed so relieved and grateful, Ellery wondered what he knew that Ellery didn't. Especially when Dylan added candidly, "I wish I could promise you won't regret it, but...you probably will."

"Oh, I know," Ellery said grimly. "Of *that*, I have zero doubt."

CHAPTER NINE

Luckily, he was in good shape because, even so, Ellery was out of breath and sweating by the time he jogged back to the Crow's Nest to grab his car. He quietly cursed both September and Dylan as he started the VW's engine.

The VW zipped through the narrow streets of the village, winding up the hillside as street lamps winked on.

September was renting a place two streets over from Jack's, which Ellery hadn't realized until that evening. When he pulled up in front of the yellow and white bungalow, all the lights were off and the curtains were closed. September's golf cart sat in the front drive, but she did not appear to be home.

Unless she'd gone to bed early?

Maybe the entire point of this exercise was to enjoy dragging Dylan away from the festival for nothing more than the pleasure of making him jump through hoops. That scenario made more sense to Ellery than one where September knowingly risked her life.

But Dylan seemed sincerely worried, and he knew September better than Ellery.

It was not the kind of thing he wanted to be wrong about, so Ellery turned off the engine and got out of the car. Cozy lights shone in the windows of the neighboring houses. It was a quiet street. Down the hill, he could see the deep blue of the harbor and the distant glow of the lamp at North Point lighthouse.

And, *very* faintly, he could hear what sounded like a dog's shrill bark carried on the sea breeze.

"Yikes," he murmured. "Surely not."

He strode briskly up the brick walkway to the front door and rang the bell.

He was not surprised when nothing happened.

He rang the bell again, but he couldn't hear it ring, so maybe it wasn't working. He tried knocking on the door.

Again, there was no response.

He sighed, took a step back to study the front of the cottage. On the roof, a whale weather vane spun aimlessly in the wind. The shutters creaked.

It was tempting to wash his hands of the situation and phone the police. Maybe the embarrassment of having Pirate's Cove's finest darkening her doorstep would put an end to September's games. The problem was, that solution would be equally embarrassing for Dylan, which is why he hadn't gone that route in the first place. Ellery understood only too well. It was no fun being the object of village gossip.

Well, no fun being the object of any gossip, really.

He checked his phone. It was now nearly eight o'clock. Hard to believe September would go to bed this early, even to make a point. It was equally hard to believe she'd be sitting in the dark, waiting for Dylan to show up. Unless she really was a sociopath, which...maybe.

He returned to the front door and knocked so hard the wreath of shell and twigs bounced. "September? Are you in there? It's Ellery."

The stubborn silence persisted.

As much as he didn't want to be any more involved than he already was, what if something *had* happened to her? What if she *had* done something stupid?

Ellery walked around the side of the bungalow to a small cement courtyard with a variety of potted plants and an iron bench. He knocked on the back door.

Nobody home.

The curtains to what was likely the bedroom were not pulled tight. He climbed onto the bench—hoping none of September's neighbors chose that moment to look out their windows—and tried to peer through the opening. As he searched for recognizable shapes within the dimness, he hoped with all his heart that September was not taking a nap and about to wake to the sight of him looming outside her window.

The interior was even darker than the surrounding night.

He hopped down and went back to the door, trying to see beneath the scalloped bottom of the curtain.

In the gloom, he could just make out the outline of table and chairs—and maybe a tiny flickering light? A candle on the table?

Tentatively, he tried the doorknob. To his surprise, the knob turned. He opened the door, but then caution—instinct?—held him motionless.

"Hello?" Ellery called from the doorstep. "September?"

He did *not* like the feel of the silence on the other side of the door.

"Please don't let this be..." He didn't finish the thought. Using his forearm, he pushed the door wide. The string of patio lights from the neighboring yard cast a baleful sheen across the scene. Ellery's uneasy gaze moved from table to sink to floor; he could hear a soft, but steady drip onto the tile. He swallowed, turned on his phone's flashlight, and directed it into the kitchen.

To his relief, he saw that water was dripping from the sink counter.

That was *much* better than the grisly explanation his imagination had supplied, but he still couldn't shake the feeling that something was very wrong.

"September?" he asked doubtfully.

He held his phone out as though trying to get a better signal. His effort to expand the range of his cell's flashlight was rewarded, if you could call it that, by the sight of something bundled in the doorway leading from the kitchen into the room beyond: a pile of filmy draperies which gradually resolved itself into a white huddled...

Pile of laundry, he told himself, and did not believe it for an instant.

His heart bounced around his chest like radar pinging off incoming trouble as his horrified gaze slowly, reluctantly picked out the shape of an outstretched hand.

"Oh God."

She wasn't bluffing. She did it.

He retreated hastily to call for help, and the slide of light briefly illuminated the gleam of something silver on the table. Not a utensil. Not a knife. Nothing that belonged on a kitchen table.

Was that—? What *was* that?

A hammer.

He blinked, trying to get his shocked brain to compute.

The hammer was out of place in that scene. Nobody used a hammer to...

"Oh *no*."

Ellery stumbled away from the door and collapsed onto the iron bench. He took a couple of deep, trembly breaths. The damp night smelled of geranium, scented candle, and the relentless creep of something coppery and sinister. He pressed Jack's number.

Jack's cell rang once and then Jack, sounding blessedly normal, said, "How goes it?"

"It's gone better," Ellery said shakily. "I'm over at September's. I think she's dead."

"What?"

"Someone's dead, anyway. I think it must be her."

"You're not making sense. Are you sure she's dead?"

Ellery closed his eyes considering the stillness, the silence, the scent of that which made your scalp prickle and your blood turn cold.

"Yes. That is, I'm pretty sure. I didn't go inside. Which, I don't know, maybe I should make sure she's not..."

Jack said sharply, *"No.* Don't go inside. Did you drive over?"

"Yes."

"Wait in your car. I'm on my way."

It seemed a lifetime before Ellery heard the sirens, saw the red and blue flash of LED bar lights speeding up the street toward where he sat shivering in his car.

Three police SUVs parked along the street. Jack got out and directed the other officers toward the house. The people in the surrounding cottages came outside, standing on their porches, hugging themselves, watching.

Jack crossed to Ellery, who had climbed out of the VW.

"Are you okay?"

Ellery nodded, reached for Jack, who wrapped his arms around him. "I don't think she killed herself."

Jack drew back, trying to read Ellery's face. "Why would she kill herself? What are you even doing here?"

"She was threatening to kill herself. But...I don't think that's what happened." Ellery dropped his forehead on Jack's shoulder. "You'd think I'd be used to this by now."

He felt Jack shake his head. "This isn't something you get used to. It isn't something you *should* get used to." His arms tightened around Ellery for a moment, then he said briskly, "Wait in your car. I'll be back in a few minutes."

Ellery nodded, folded back in the VW, watching as Jack disappeared around the back of the bungalow. He resumed his internal debate on whether to phone Dylan.

If their positions were reversed, he'd want to know as soon as possible. But this was not the first time he'd stumbled onto a crime scene. He knew how this worked. How it was supposed to work, anyway, and he knew Jack would not approve, might even interpret a phone call to Dylan the wrong way. So he sat still and silent, watching the beam of flashlights poking around the exterior of the house and then retreating inside to move with ominous deliberation behind the curtains and blinds.

Eventually, a black Infiniti Q60 pulled up behind Ellery's car and the tall, well-built figure of Dr. Robert Mane got out. Rob, medical director and CEO of the Buck Island Med Center, operated as the island's ME pro tempore when the official medical examiner in Providence couldn't make it to an island crime scene in a timely manner.

Rob walked up to Ellery's car, tapped on the VW's window. Ellery rolled the window down.

"I don't want to say this is starting to look suspicious..." Rob said.

"Yeah, please don't say that."

Rob made a sound of amusement, but said, "I thought you were going to give me a call this week?"

"Sorry. The past few days have been crazy."

"Sure. I know. Sherlock Holmes had the same problem." Robert's fingers tapped out a fleeting *toodeloo* on the window, and he continued on his way, disappearing around the back of the bungalow.

The minutes ticked slowly by.

Eventually Jack came around the back of the cottage, ducked beneath the crime scene tape stretched across the driveway, and climbed into the VW.

Ellery said, "Is she—?"

"Yes."

Jack gazed at Ellery in the gloom, and then asked the inevitable question, the question Ellery had been dreading. "What exactly were you doing here, Ell?"

"Dylan got a weird phone message from September. He was afraid she might harm herself, but he didn't think it was a good idea to come himself."

"So he sent you over here." Jack's tone was without inflection.

"Yes."

Jack watched a Med Center ambulance back into the driveway. "Did you hear the message from September?"

Ellery's, "Yes," was more tentative than he'd intended.

"Yes?"

Ellery nodded.

Jack said quietly, "Ellery."

Ellery said earnestly, "Jack, listen. Remember when I got that message from Brandon asking for help? But everyone else who heard it couldn't make out what he was saying—"

Jack interjected, "You mean the message Brandon didn't actually send?"

Funny how he still remembered that call as coming from Brandon. It took Ellery a moment to recover his thoughts. "But there *was* a message. That's my point."

As usual Jack went straight to the heart of the matter. "Are you sure it was September you heard leaving that message? Could you—*would* you swear to it in court?"

"Swear to it in court?" Ellery echoed.

"Yes."

"I'm sure it was September. But I'm not—it was difficult to understand what she was saying."

"I see."

Ellery tried to read Jack's expression in the gloom. "If you're thinking Dylan had any part of this, you're wrong."

Instead of answering, Jack pulled out his cell phone. "I'm going to tape your statement now. I want you to tell me everything that happened after you left the Salty Dog up to when you phoned me."

Tersely, matching Jack's tone, Ellery went through his steps after paying for their meal at the pub.

Jack only interrupted twice. Once to ask about Dylan's demeanor when he'd approached Ellery. Once to ask why Ellery hadn't phoned the police when September didn't answer the doorbell.

The first question was easy enough to answer.

"Dylan seemed honestly worried. Which is why I agreed to come over here. His reasons for not coming himself made sense to me."

Jack reserved comment on that one.

The second question was trickier.

"I didn't phone the police because I wasn't one hundred percent sure September's threat was authentic."

"In fact, you weren't sure there *was* a threat because you couldn't make out most of the message purportedly left by her."

Ellery did not like Jack's tone and the use of the word *purported* felt hostile. "If it was just emotional black-mail, then phoning the police would teach her a lesson, but it would also be humiliating for Dylan. And it would be a waste of police resources when your team was already stretched thin."

Jack snorted. "Come off it."

"I'm just telling you what ran through my mind. If a po-lice report got filed, how long before a story popped up in the *Scuttlebutt Weekly* about a police incident occurring at Dylan Carter's girlfriend's house?"

That time, Jack said nothing.

"I didn't think September was the self-harming type. I figured she was trying to manipulate Dylan. She's been badmouthing him all over the village. I didn't want to help her smear his reputation. But I couldn't be one hundred per cent sure it wasn't a-a cry for help. Which is why I didn't leave."

"You went around to the back of the cottage," prompted Jack.

Ellery finished recounting his discovery of September's body.

"Did you step inside the cottage?"

"No."

"Are you sure?"

"Positive."

"You didn't touch anything but the bench, the window, and the door handle?"

"Correct."

"Okay." Jack clicked his phone, reached for the car door. "You're still heading over to my place? I won't be home until late."

"Jack, you haven't even said what happened. *Was* she murdered?"

Jack glanced back; his expression indecipherable. "Yes. She was murdered."

He had been expecting it, so why was it such a shock?

"How?"

"The back of her head was bashed in with a hammer she'd been using to break up a block of ice." He added bleakly, "She was in the process of mixing cocktails."

For a shocked moment, Ellery couldn't think past the unlikelihood of September being murdered.

No, she was not a very nice person. But to *kill* her?

She's the most unlikeable woman I've ever known.

He gathered his wits, said quickly, "Jack, Dylan didn't do this."

"I'll talk to you tomorrow morning."

"Jack—"

Jack swung the car door shut, cutting off the rest of Ellery's words.

"Are you freaking kidding me?" In disbelief, Ellery watched Jack stride up the drive, duck under the crime scene tape, and disappear around the back of the bungalow.

For a few seconds, Ellery fumed. Then, once again, he debated phoning Dylan, this time to warn him.

But there was no question that, at this juncture, Jack would view that as disloyalty—if not high treason. As dismayed as Ellery was by Jack's suspicions, and as outraged as he was by Jack's highhanded behavior, he couldn't betray Jack's trust.

He started the Volkswagen, drew carefully past the additional emergency vehicles pulling up at the bungalow, and made the short drive back to Jack's cottage.

There, Watson was ready and waiting to share his own views on the topics of trust, loyalty, and high treason.

"I know," Ellery told him. "I *know*. But I can't take you *every*where."

Watson disagreed, and offered many loud if not logical reasons to support his argument.

Ellery did his best to soothe his little pal's injured feelings with cuddles, and eventually Watson allowed him to make up for his transgressions by throwing the raggedy remnants of what had once been a squeaky lamb toy, until Ellery's arm was ready to fall off.

After Watson had worked out his frustrations with the world in general and Ellery in particular, they retreated to the kitchen where Ellery fixed himself a cup of tea and troubledly studied his silent phone.

He understood why Jack had to consider Dylan a suspect. Boyfriends, girlfriends, husbands, wives, romantic and domestic partners of any and all stripes were *always* the initial suspect in the violent death of a significant other. Until Jack could clear Dylan, he had to consider him a person of interest.

Ellery also understood why Jack wasn't going to discuss the case with *him* before he'd even finished his preliminary investigation.

He understood, but it was still worrying.

Nearly as worrying as the fact that Dylan hadn't bothered to phone him once to learn what had happened after Ellery got to September's bungalow.

CHAPTER TEN

It was after four in the morning when Jack finally, finally got home.

By then, Ellery had long given up waiting for him, and he didn't even wake to the sound of Jack's key in the front door lock. Even Watson could barely rouse himself to more than a few sleepy snuffles of welcome when Jack finally came to bed. Ellery, who had been dreaming he was auditioning for a dog food commercial—wearing a black dog suit, no less—wordlessly drew back the blankets and reached for Jack.

Jack fell into bed beside him, resting his head against Ellery's. "I'm glad you stayed," he muttered. "I wasn't sure you would."

"Of course I stayed." Ellery kissed him. Jack kissed him back.

It was very late and they were very tired, but that seemed to cover the essentials. They fell asleep in each other's arms.

In the morning, however, things were different.

Ellery was determined to talk to Jack about the case in general and Dylan in particular, but he knew he had to pick his moment. Aggravatingly, the moment didn't come. Jack was careful, courteous, and clearly couldn't wait to get out of the house and away from Ellery.

"You're not staying for breakfast?" Ellery pushed back the shower curtain when Jack popped open the bathroom door to say he was leaving.

"No time."

"No time for a cup of coffee?"

Jack held up his insulated mug by way of answer.

Ellery shook his wet hair out of his eyes. "You don't have to flee your residence, Jack. I wasn't going to grill you. I just want to know if you questioned Dylan last night. Or do I have to rely on Nora for my updates?" He was partly kidding. Partly not.

Either way, Jack was not amused.

His jaw got as square and uncordial as a NO TRESPASS-ING sign. "We interviewed Dylan. We haven't made an arrest. But you should know—and this is not public information—"

Oops. Maybe not the best choice of words. Ellery, who had spent the prior evening struggling with torn loyalties, went from slight exasperation to full out ire in less than a second.

"You think I don't know that!"

Jack gave him a cool look, and finished, "—Dylan's our prime suspect."

"That's ridiculous."

"Is it?"

"You *know* it is."

Jack began to tick off his bullet points. "Dylan and September had numerous public arguments over the past week. September repeatedly claimed that Dylan was controlling and abusive."

"Does that sound like Dylan to you?" Ellery interrupted.

But Jack would not be interrupted. "Dylan was overheard telling Tom Tulley he'd like to wring September's neck. Not once, which would be bad enough. On *two* separate occasions."

"Yeah, but her neck wasn't..." Ellery swallowed. "Wrung."

"He argued with her again hours before he received a garbled, all but incomprehensible phone message that he *claims* was September threatening suicide, and then he sent *you* over there to conveniently discover her body."

Ellery was smart enough to see that Dylan sending *him* to September's was an especially black mark in Jack's book. It defused some of his aggravation.

He said more patiently, "People argue, Jack. We're arguing right now. Dylan wouldn't have sent me over there, if he'd killed her. I'm telling you; he wouldn't have done that to me."

Jack shook his head impatiently, as though Ellery just didn't get it. And really, is there anything more irritating than someone implying you don't know enough to know what's good for you?

"He admitted last night that he's been trying to end the relationship for the past month, but she kept dragging him back in."

"It's not like she could have held him prisoner. They were having a messy breakup. Believe me, it happens. It usually doesn't end in murder."

"Sometimes it does. And this looks like one of those times."

"He didn't do it. He can't be your *main* suspect."

Jack met his gaze straight on. "Ellery, he's our *only* suspect."

"Well, you're wrong," Ellery said. "Again."

Which was definitely not the most tactful thing *he* could have said, but he wasn't used to Jack coming at him like a steamroller. Maybe Jack was hoping to quash any rebellion before it got started, but maybe he just really, *really* hated arguing with Ellery as much as Ellery hated arguing with him. Whichever, the—as it felt to Ellery—Totalitarian Dictator approach put his back up big time.

Jack's blue-green eyes narrowed. His mouth tightened. "I think it's a good idea we avoid discussing this particular case."

"Speak for yourself."

"I *am* speaking for myself." Jack seemed to struggle inwardly. "You think I'm enjoying this? Dylan's my friend, too. I don't want to believe he killed his girlfriend, but that's how the facts are stacking up. And that's what I have to go by. Not your feelings. Not my feelings. *The facts.*"

That was painful, but it made sense. Ellery was silent. Unfortunately, Jack added, "And you're not helping."

Uh. Oh.

"You got it. We won't discuss it again." Ellery yanked the shower curtain back into place.

Over the rush of water came a very loud silence on the other side of the plastic curtain. Then the curtain gusted and blew back as the bathroom door silently closed.

Despite the brisk and beautiful weather, Ellery, unsurprisingly, was not in the best of moods when he arrived to open the Crow's Nest a short time later—and the sight of the Silver Sleuths already gathered around the sales desk did little to help.

Nora spotted him and demanded, "*Where* on earth have you been?" As though Ellery worked for her instead of (in theory) the other way around.

Watson, however, was delighted to see his fans and supporters ready to greet him, and he snatched his leash right out of Ellery's hand, galloping up the center aisle to say his hellos.

Arf. Arf. Arf.

He was immediately treated to bits of breakfast sandwich, bagels, and blintzes, which he wolfed down as though he hadn't eaten in weeks.

"He's getting so big!" Edna exclaimed.

"Just about the size of a giant rat," agreed Mr. Starling, who seemed recovered from his spell in dry dock.

Mrs. Ferris, despite being a cat person, cooed, "Who could resist those eyes?" And handed over another bit of breakfast sandwich to Watson who was all but batting his eyelashes.

Ellery swallowed his exasperation, pushing the door shut against the brisk wind blowing from the harbor. The sea breeze was so strong it shook the tall case enclosing Rupert, the pirate-garbed resin skeleton who served as the bookshop's mascot. The glass rippled as though Rupert was about to break out of his see-through tomb. And given the way Ellery's day was going—.

His gaze fell on a square white envelope at the foot of the display.

ELLERY PAGE was printed in big, childlike letters.

His heart sank. Every time he thought his poison pen pal had moved onto more interesting subjects, another one of these greetings from the Twilight Zone showed up.

He felt around in his pocket for the small roll of plastic waste bags he kept on hand for Watson's convenience, tore off a green bag printed with tiny paw prints, and gingerly picked up the corner of the envelope.

"Dearie, what are you *doing*? You're late for your photoshoot!" Nora cried.

At the same moment, Hermione announced, "Someone tried to kill Lara Fairplay last night!"

Ellery dropped the envelope. His head shot up. "*What* did you say?"

Nora made shushing motions to Hermione. "Don't distract him with that now." To Ellery, she said, "She's *fine*. The stage trap door gave way last night during her performance."

Ellery's heart stopped. "She fell? Was she hurt?"

"No, no. It's all right. She didn't fall. It could even have been an accident."

"Tosh!" Stanley said.

"Of course it couldn't!" Hermione sounded indignant at the very idea of *accidents* happening in their village.

Nora glared at them both. "It can *wait* till he gets back," she insisted. "He *can't* miss this."

"Miss what? Get back from where? What the hel-heck is going on?" Ellery protested.

"The Gentlemen of Note calendar for the village widows-and-orphans fund. The photoshoot is this morning." With silent, Jeeves-like efficiency, Kingston appeared, seemingly out of thin air, beside Ellery. He took the plastic bag from Ellery, retrieved the envelope, and said quietly, "Would you like me to put this in your desk drawer?"

All that was missing was a butler-esque *sir*.

Ellery stared into Kingston's shrewd green eyes. "Uh... Yes. Thanks."

"They've phoned twice asking where you are," Nora said. "You *have* to go."

Ellery groaned. He'd forgotten completely about the calendar photoshoot. He'd forgotten completely that he'd ever agreed to do that idiotic calendar.

"Where am I going?"

"The Seacrest Inn."

"The—oh." He broke off as an idea occurred to him.

"Which is very convenient," Nora agreed. "Because when you're done having your picture taken, you can have a word with our client."

"**B**eautiful! Beautiful!" crowed the high school photographer wielding the three-thousand-dollar Canon EOS R6. "*Bellissimo!*"

The kid, whose name Ellery had already forgotten, leaped goatlike over the lichen-encrusted boulders, landing on the outcropping above Ellery to dangle precariously overhead, snapping pics like the paparazzi had stormed the beaches of Buck Island.

"Glorious! That's right. Soak up the sun. Tilt your chin. Bathe in that heavenly light. You're sunbathing on the shores of St. Mary's Island thinking about all that pirate...booty."

Ellery opened his eyes. The kid—seventeen maybe? No more than eighteen at the most—grinned down at him and winked.

"Now brood! Brood for me, baby! It's a dark and stormy night, and your ship is going down fast."

Ellery laughed.

The maniac with the camera laughed too and let the camera shutter fly.

Unlike most of Pirate's Cove's "Gentlemen of Note," Ellery had a lot of experience with photoshoots—though rarely had he been shot by a hyperactive teen photog on a windswept cliff overlooking the ocean. But it seemed the professional photographer usually hired for this event had gone out of business, so in desperation the town council had turned to the talents of the president of the high school photography club.

Anyway, it was an easy enough gig and at least Ellery got to keep his clothes on—or rather the costume donated by the Scallywags, Pirate's Cove's local amateur theater guild. As a matter of fact, he had worn these breeches, green-gold silk waistcoat and black velvet frock coat to the Marauder's Masquerade in July.

Poor Captain August, on the other hand, was clambering over the rocks bare-chested and barefooted in his flatteringly fitted breeches and goosebumps as Ellery headed back to the changing room inside the inn.

Captain June had seemingly come and gone. Jack was supposed to be lined up as Captain July, but Ellery was pretty sure Jack had more important things on his mind than beefcake calendars and camera angles.

One of those things would surely be Captain November AKA Dylan, who showed up as Ellery was climbing back into this jeans, T-shirt, and sweater in the conference room temporarily serving as a changing room.

"Ahoy," Dylan said. Despite his cheery demeanor, Dylan looked haggard. There were dark shadows beneath his eyes and lines around his mouth that had never been there before.

"Hey. I wondered if you'd be here. Are you all right?"

"I should be asking you that." Dylan threw a hunted look at the door. "Can we talk?"

"Of course. Now?"

"No. Can you meet me at my house around one?" Dylan added bitterly, "Assuming, I haven't already been arrested."

Ellery said quickly, "Don't say that."

Dylan's eyes glittered with a mix of emotions. "One o'clock?"

Ellery nodded. "One."

He finished dressing, left the changing room, and made his way through the inn's crowded lobby. It seemed the Sing the Plank festival was good for one local business at least.

He headed upstairs to the suite where Lara was staying.

Halfway up the stairs, he met Jane Smith on her way down.

Jane jumped as if at the sight of a ghost. "*Oh*! Ellery! I didn't expect to see you here."

Likewise, but Ellery said pleasantly, "Hi Jane. How's Lara this morning?"

Jane shook her head. "They're *very* upset with you. I don't think it's a good idea to go up right now. Mr. Neilson is talking about suing you."

Ellery's heart dropped. "Suing *me*? For what?"

"You were supposed to make sure nothing happened to Lara. It's sheer chance she wasn't killed last night. You didn't go to the concert. You weren't even in the theater. I'm honestly shocked that you'd just...just blow off a case!"

Jane did seem genuinely perturbed about it. Her face was flushed and her eyes were pink as though she'd been crying.

"I didn't blow anything off," Ellery protested.

"Well, where were you?" Jane asked, which was a fair question.

"Something came up."

Jane stared at him. "*Ohhhh*," she said wisely. "Poor Mr. Carter. Such a nice man, I always thought. Such nice manners. You can never tell though. Not that he has to worry. She was an outsider, after all. *He's* a respected member of the community."

Oh no. Was that what people thought? That September wouldn't get justice because she was "an outsider?" That Dylan would get off, not because he was innocent, but because he was a respected member of the community?

"Dylan didn't kill September. He would never hurt anyone."

Jane gave a tight smile. "You're so loyal to your friends. Not *all* your friends, of course."

That was definitely pointed. "What's that mean?"

"You weren't very loyal to *me*." Jane shrugged. "I suppose you thought you were being loyal to Nora."

"I wasn't aware there was a contest between you."

"There's always a contest when Nora's involved. Anyway, you know what they say, choose your friends wisely and your enemies *more* wisely."

"I'm pretty sure that's not what they say."

"Isn't it? Oh well. I did warn you." Jane delivered another of those pinched smiles and trotted past him down the staircase.

Ellery stared after her. He wasn't imagining it, right? That had definitely been one strange encounter.

He continued more slowly up to Lara's suite.

To recap, his morning was off to a fairly terrible start.

He'd quarreled with Jack, learned his best friend was about to be arrested for murder, received another poison pen letter, smeared spray tan on his T-shirt and makeup on his favorite black sweater, received cryptic threats from Jane Smith—and it was not even eleven o'clock yet.

What next?

He didn't have to wait long to find out.

As he reached the second floor, Lara's suite door opened and Neilson Elon stepped into the hallway. He bristled at the sight of Ellery, and closed the door with a bang.

"What's this supposed to be?" he demanded. "Better late than never?"

Ellery did not like confrontation. He was getting better at dealing with it, out of self-preservation, but his instinct was still to avoid it when possible. However, as previously established, he'd had a hell of a morning, and he surprised both himself and Neilson by planting his hands on his hips and saying pugnaciously, "Look, I'm not a bodyguard and I made that clear at the outset."

Neilson matched his aggressive posture and raised his voice. "No, you're not a bodyguard, but you were supposed to find out who was behind these threats so we wouldn't *need* a bodyguard."

"That's *another* thing: you've *got* your own security. How is it my fault that your security team didn't do their job?"

"They *did* do their job, which is why Lara isn't lying in the hospital with a broken back. Or worse. No thanks to you!"

"I've had barely forty-eight hours to work on this. You sat on those threats for how long? Nor did you give me a whole lot of anything to work with. The *only* person who's been willing to talk to me is Lara, and I think it's pretty clear you're not telling her everything."

Neilson's eyes narrowed. He said dangerously, "What are you getting at?"

It seemed like a strangely defensive response. What did he think Ellery was suggesting?

Ellery said, "Lara's take is you're trying to protect her. To not bother her with things that might distract from making her comeback."

Neilson's shoulders relaxed. He stopped looking like he was ready to throw a punch. "That's right. That's *exactly* right. We're trying to pull off a show here. You know how much time and organization and effort that requires?"

"I've got a pretty good idea."

That was clearly not the right answer. Neilson's lip curled. "The hell you do."

"The point is, I've got to have more to work with in order to do what you want me to do."

Neilson's mouth curled into a sneer. "Thanks, but no thanks. We don't need your help from here on out."

Frankly, it was a relief. The money, though always welcome, wasn't as necessary as it had been several hours and fifty thousand dollars earlier, and Ellery already had more on his plate than he could deal with. Responsibility for someone else's safety was a side dish too far.

"Okay." he shrugged. "Fine with me. I haven't liked this set up from the start."

Neilson again assumed that belligerent posture. "Oh really?"

"Yes, really."

Neilson started to reply, but the suite door opened and Jocasta, Lara's sister, slipped outside.

She hissed, "Will you two shut up? Lara's trying to write."

The silence that followed her words was broken was by muffled guitar chords.

Neilson pointed at Ellery. "He just quit."

Jocasta gasped, swung on Ellery, "*Why*? After last night? How could you!"

Ellery gave Neilson a look of disgust. "I didn't quit. He said my services were no longer needed."

"*Neil.*"

"Neil what?" Neilson protested. "He wasn't even there last night, Jo. He couldn't even bother to show up."

"I did show up. I had to leave."

Neilson put his hands up like, *what did I tell you?*

Jocasta got in front of Ellery, pleading, "Don't quit. At least...give me five minutes and if you still want to quit after that, okay. But we really do need help." She threw an impatient look at her brother-in-law. "After last night, we've *got* to have help, Neil. You know it as well as I do."

"If *he's* your idea of help, we're all doomed."

Probably. It was kind of hard to argue, given his current batting average, but Ellery ignored Nielson and said to Jocasta, "If you want to talk, we can talk. It certainly would have been helpful on Thursday, if someone had told me what the actual deal was. But I still think, especially after last night, you should go to the police."

"*No cops!*" Neilson exclaimed.

"*Shhhh!*" Jocasta fastened her hand on Ellery's arm. "Come on," she coaxed, drawing him away from the door. "We can discuss downstairs."

Ellery threw a final, doubtful look at the door to Lara's suite, and followed Jocasta downstairs.

.

CHAPTER ELEVEN

The cafe was crowded seemingly to capacity, but it turned out membership really did have its privileges. Ellery and "Call Me Jo" hadn't long to wait before they were led to a small booth in the sunny greenhouse style dining room.

As soon as they were done with the business of ordering their coffee and food, Jocasta said earnestly, "I'm sorry about Neil. He's under so much pressure. We're all just *really* stressed. We were hoping to get a lot more media coverage, but so far there's been nothing. *Zilch.*"

Hearing that *zilch* wouldn't exactly make Sue Lewis's day.

Ellery said, "Saturday's the big night, right? So maybe tonight—"

"I've been trying to get hold of every contact I have at every music mag still in existence. Lara was on the cover of *Rolling Stone twice*, but they're not even returning my phone calls. It's not *fair.*"

First rule of show business: Life was not fair.

"I'm sorry."

"You'd think between Stephen Foster and Lara Fairplay, someone would be interested!"

Gosh, it sounded like Stephen Foster's reps weren't pulling their weight! But, of course, Ellery kept that thought to himself. "You'd think," he said neutrally.

"And then all the threats. And *now* all these accidents! Shouldn't that be a story in itself?"

Ellery studied Jocasta's face. Did she understand what she'd just said? "I thought you were keeping a lid on that? That you and the festival organizers didn't want word getting out about threats against Lara."

Jocasta looked like she didn't understand. "If something happens, it's not like we can hide it."

The waitress arrived with their breakfasts. Ellery's brows shot up. He had a healthy appetite, but Jocasta had ordered enough food to feed half their road crew. Maybe she—

Nope. Jocasta picked up her fork and dived right into that stack of blueberry pancakes.

As the much-impressed waitress moved away, Ellery said, "Well, right. About last night's accident—"

Jocasta lowered her fork. "No, it's okay. We heard about Mr. Carter's girlfriend. And that you were there when it happened."

"Well, not exact—"

"Nobody's blaming you for last night. It could even have been an accident."

Yeah, *nobody* thought it was an accident. That '*could even have been*' was a dead giveaway.

"Maybe." Ellery sincerely doubted it. He knew for a fact the trapdoor had been nailed shut after the previous year's close call. Still, the theater and stage were long due for an overhaul. Maybe it *was* possible something had broken loose. "What exactly happened?"

"Lara was right in the middle of 'Fool Me, Fool You,' and the trap door just…opened. It fell open. She moves around a lot on stage so, luckily, she wasn't standing squarely on it. She almost lost her balance, but caught herself and stepped back." Jocasta added proudly, "She didn't even miss a beat."

"The show didn't stop?"

"Nope. Mr. Carter and the stage crew ran down there and shored it up again. I don't think most of the audience even knew what happened." She swallowed. "What nearly happened."

He'd have to talk to Dylan and get his take, but two close calls, two maybe-accidents in twenty-four hours seemed like a lot.

"Your security guys didn't have anything to do with preventing Lara's fall? Because your brother-in-law said the only reason she wasn't in the hospital was thanks to your security team."

Jocasta's sigh seemed weary beyond her years. "Neil's just saying what he wishes was true. He wants to be Lara's knight in shining armor. He couldn't protect her before, so he wants her to see he's protecting her now."

Maybe? Ellery hadn't been keen on Neilson before the run-in upstairs, and he was even less keen now. But just because he didn't like the guy, didn't mean Neilson wasn't doing the best he could with the tools he had.

"Okay, well, our agreement was that if I came to the conclusion that Lara's life was in danger, you'd go to the police—"

"That's not going to happen," Jocasta interrupted.

"But—"

"I know that's what we said, but Lara was never on board with that. There's no way."

"That doesn't make sense. I understand Lara has some hard feelings—"

"No. You don't. I'm not saying it's logical. Lara *hates* the police. She hates them and she's afraid of them. If you'd known her before... But everything changed after Dawn Shumway."

"Dawn Shumway is the woman who died in the bar fight?"

The lines of Jocasta's face tightened. "See, that's the first misconception right there. That it was a bar fight. It wasn't. It happened in a hotel dining room. Lara just happened to be having a drink before dinner. She was sitting at a table with one of her backup singers and Gig, the drummer. Dawn Shumway came up to them and started harassing Lara. It wasn't the first time. She'd been accusing Lara of stealing her songs for years. She was always threatening to sue, and Lara was like, *Let her.* Lara wasn't stealing Dawn's music. She'd never heard of Dawn until Dawn started writing all those crazy letters. Nobody took it seriously. Which was a mistake."

"Yes." Probably. But Ellery had done the same thing with the letters he received from crackpots. It wasn't until the threats were hand delivered, he'd started to take them seriously, and largely that was because Jack took them seriously.

"That evening was different. Dawn pulled out a knife. Dawn *brought a knife* to confront Lara. I don't know why that didn't mean anything at the trial. Dawn attacked Lara. Right there in the dining room. Lara grabbed for the knife, they struggled, and Lara ended up stabbing Dawn. That's how fast it happened. Lara didn't plan on it. She didn't want to do that. She was defending herself. It wasn't a knife fight or a bar fight. Not the way they made it sound. Lara was accosted by a stalker whom she killed while defending herself."

"Then why—"

Jocasta burst out, "Because of 'Blue Street Blues.'"

Clearly that was supposed to mean something to Ellery. "The TV show?"

"That's *Hill Street Blues*. 'Blue Street Blues' is one of Laura's best-known songs."

"I'm not really familiar with a lot of Lara's work," he said apologetically.

Jocasta gave him a look of disbelief. "You never heard 'Blue Street Blues?'"

"I've probably heard it. I just don't remember it."

Jocasta rolled her eyes. "It's a song about the police murdering a young black musician."

"Ah. I see." Not a number likely to pop up on Jack's Greatest Songs Ever playlist, that was for sure.

"It's a political protest song. It's an *anthem*."

"Right. Got it."

"And it's a true story. Lara knew the kid."

"So you think the police had it in for Lara because she wrote a song that was critical to law enforcement?"

"It wasn't just the one song. She wrote 'Friday Night in Fresno,' 'The Boy from Chino Hills,' 'Bobby Mack Does Smack'... The cops investigating Dawn Shumway's death were biased. *Lara* was the victim, but from the very start they treated *her* like the aggressor. That attitude was reflected in the report they wrote and the way they presented the case to the DA."

"Okay, I guess I understand why Lara doesn't want to go to the police. Couldn't she hire an actual bodyguard? Because, no disrespect to your road crew, they're not really trained to provide security. They're more like bouncers, right?"

Jocasta nodded. "It's just...money's tight. A *real* bodyguard, like a *celebrity* bodyguard? That can cost more than a hundred dollars an hour. We're hoping we don't really need that level of skill and training."

It seemed to Ellery that after the incident with Dawn Shumway, cutting corners would be a non-starter for Lara and her family. But he also knew what it was like to have to pinch your pennies even when it came down to the essentials.

As if Jocasta read his mind, she added, "We're hoping that if the threat is real, it's specific to Lara coming back to Pirate's Cove. That we won't have to worry about it after we leave the island on Sunday night."

That sounded more like they were resigned to spending the weekend dodging bullets rather than counting on him to solve the mystery of who was sending Lara death threats. Which was frankly a relief. At the same time...

"Two near-fatal accidents in the space of twenty-four hours worries me."

"I know, but really, how would a bodyguard have helped in either of those of cases? It's an old theater. You said so yourself. The light falling and the trap door opening could really be accidents."

"They could, but there could also be a pattern of attempts made to look like accidents."

"I know."

This territory was always thin ice, and Ellery proceeded with caution. "Is there anyone else who might have a grudge against Lara? How does she get along with the rest of the band?"

"They're not really a band. They're just back up players. Hired guns. With the exception of Gig, the drummer. Gig's been with Lara since White Wine Records." Jocasta gave a little laugh at Ellery's expression. "In fairness, Lara's band never was a band so much as regular backup players. No one ever got a vote on anything. Lara *was* the band."

"I see."

"But she's really good to her players. She insists that we pay them well—more than we can afford, honestly. They're in the same hotel as us. You don't have to worry about the band."

"Check. Next question. Why did Lara cut Neilson out of her will when she went to prison?"

Jocasta's eyes widened. "She told you that?"

Ellery nodded.

Jocasta bit her lip, stared out the window. Clearly this presented a dilemma for her, and Ellery thought he knew why. Jocasta was a loyal sister, but she seemed pretty darned fond of her brother-in-law.

She said finally, "Lara felt like Neil didn't fight hard enough to keep her from going to jail."

"Oh." Not what Ellery expected.

"Also, he was having an affair."

"*Oh*." *That* was what Ellery expected.

"The affairs didn't mean anything," Jocasta said quickly.

"Affair*s*. Like plural?"

Jocasta nodded. "Neil was a player before they got married. I mean a *playa* player, not a musician. Anyway, it took him a while to settle down. Lara knew and she didn't care. She was crazy about him. And she knew he was crazy about her. But then, when she realized she was really going to go to prison, she got paranoid. She changed her will. But she changed it back when she got out."

Had she? A lot had happened since his breakfast meeting with Lara, but Ellery's impression was Lara had *not* changed her will back. He distinctly remembered her saying everything went to Jocasta.

Then again, Lara had also said that both Neilson and Jocasta knew the terms of her will, and it was clear Jocasta did not.

"She's different now," Jocasta was saying. "If you'd known her before... She was a different person. I mean, she was always driven. She was never *patient*, but she didn't used to be unkind. Not deliberately."

Ellery considered that. "You think she's deliberately unkind now?"

Jocasta, too, seemed to consider. "Maybe not deliberately. That might not be fair. But now she doesn't care if she's unkind. If she hurts your feelings, she thinks it your problem. She's a lot harder. A lot more cynical. The only thing she cares about now is the music."

"It would change you, I guess. Going to prison."

"She says it gave her a lot to write about." Jocasta smiled faintly. "But it did change her. She has trouble sleeping. She doesn't like to leave her room. She can't stand crowds. Those are all problems for a musician. Yeah, it changed her. In little ways and in big ways. I miss the old Lara."

Ellery checked his phone. He didn't want to keep Dylan waiting.

"Do you have any idea who on this island could be sending those threats to Lara?"

Jocasta nibbled her bottom lip in what Ellery was recognizing as one of her giveaways. "Not really. Did Lara have any ideas?"

"She did, yeah. She mentioned being in a band with a couple of people back when your family used to summer here. That there might be some hard feelings there?"

"Jamie and Arti? Wow. She really did tell you everything."

Ellery laughed. "I seriously doubt that."

"I don't think even Neil knows. I only know because I was there when she and Arti submitted their song."

"Okay, tell me about that."

Jocasta said slowly, "Well, there isn't much to tell. The record label wanted Lara, not the song. And Lara took the deal. Arti and Jamie were disappointed, of course, but it was always going to go that way. Backsplash Butterfly wasn't even her band. She just played with them when we spent summers here. If White Wine hadn't discovered her through that dumb song, Arti and Jamie wouldn't have thought anything about her getting a deal and them not. Everybody always knew Lara was going to be famous one day."

"Did you know Arti and Jamie pretty well?"

Jocasta made a face. "I was the annoying kid sister, so not really. Jamie was always super sweet, but that's probably because he was in love with Lara. Arti didn't have the time of day for me." Almost at once, she reconsidered. "No, that's not fair." She smiled reminiscently. "Arti made me a beaded bracelet for my birthday once. And sometimes, during rehearsal breaks, she'd braid my hair."

"Did you ever see them or talk to them after Lara took the deal with White Wine Records?"

Jocasta shook her head. "I wasn't there for that band meeting. I don't think they ever spoke to her again."

"I thought you said Jamie was in love with her?"

"He was. Lara wasn't interested. She made that clear early on."

"So you never talked to either Jamie or Arti after that? You never saw them or heard from them again?"

"No." Jocasta added shortly, "I didn't ask them to send threats to my sister, if that's what you're asking."

"Of course not. Do you think they'd still hold grudges after all this time?"

Jocasta hesitated. "Is that what Lara said?"

"Lara said she thought it was unlikely."

"Same. It was decades ago. White Wine Records dumped Lara after a year. It's not like that was even her big break."

"It was her first break, though."

"Even so. I just can't see them holding onto a grudge that long. Jamie was really nice. Really sincere. He wasn't the type to send death threats. And Arti's probably married now with a bunch of kids in their own band."

"You might be surprised." Ellery glanced at his phone again and said, "I'm sorry. I've got to go. How did the debut of 'Angel Beneath the Waves' go last night?"

Jocasta shook her head. "It didn't happen. After the trap door incident, Lara cut it from the set. I think she was rattled. She stuck to the fan faves. The tried-and-true stuff. She's planning to do it tonight."

"Oh. Is that why Jane was here this morning?"

Jocasta looked blank. "Jane?"

"Jane Smith. The lady who found the Stephen Foster song."

Jocasta was still not following. "Ms. Smith? Is she staying in the inn?"

"No, I'm sure she's not. She lives in the village. I met her on the stairs just a while ago."

Jocasta's pale brows rose. "Weird. We didn't see her this morning."

CHAPTER TWELVE

Ellery could not remember ever seeing Dylan's house quiet and shuttered.

Usually there were numerous cars and golf carts parked in the shady lane in front of the charming 1950s white coastal cottage. Rarely did Ellery visit that the sound of voices and laughter, the clink of glasses did not greet him before he ever set foot on Dylan's nautical-themed welcome mat.

Today the lane was empty. The cottage was silent. The scrape of Ellery's footsteps as he jogged up the walkway of granite pavers seemed unnervingly loud.

Before he reached the small porch, the front door opened. Dylan, looking as though he hadn't slept or even changed clothes since the night before, practically yanked him inside. He hadn't shaved and his hair looked like Einstein's after a rough night of figuring out how to split atoms. "Thank God you came."

"Are you okay?"

They hugged briefly, and Dylan ushered Ellery into the long, comfortable living room with its vintage theater sign and colorful theatrical posters. "What the hell *happened* last night?"

"I got to September's house and all the lights were off—"

Dylan interrupted, "When? When did you get there?"

"It was just about eight. I went straight over after we talked."

"Of course. Yes. I'm just trying to understand…"

Good luck with that. Was murder ever something that could be fully understood?

Ellery continued, "The curtains were drawn. Her golf cart was in the driveway, so I figured she had to be there. But she didn't answer the doorbell."

"The doorbell doesn't work," Dylan said automatically.

"Right. Well, I knocked, I called her name. Then I went around to the back and tried to peek through the windows. I thought maybe she'd left a candle burning—"

"She did that all the time."

"I tried the door handle. I don't know why. I really need to stop doing that. Anyway, the door opened and I looked inside. I couldn't see much at first, but then I realized something—September—was lying in the doorway between the kitchen and, I guess, the living room."

"Did you go in? Did you…" Dylan's voice faded and he stared blankly at the picture his imagination had summoned.

Ellery shook his head. "No. I-I was pretty sure it was too late." He swallowed as his stomach roiled unhappily at the memory.

"*God*," Dylan dropped his face in his hands. "God. God. God. *Why* did this have to happen?"

"I'm really sorry, Dylan."

Dylan sat up, shaking his head. He patted Ellery's knee. "It's not… I'm going to sound utterly heartless. I'm sorry she's dead. I am. But I'm sorrier I ever got involved with her."

Ellery did not reply. He preferred Dylan's honesty to fake grief. But Dylan's honesty was dangerous, too. Not everyone was going to understand where Dylan was coming from.

"Jack thinks *I* killed her." Dylan's tone was almost wondering. "After all these years, he thinks I'm capable of murder."

"Jack thinks everyone is capable of murder," Ellery said. He couldn't help a tinge of bitterness. "Given the right set of circumstances."

Dylan stared at him with bloodshot eyes. "These would not have been the right set of circumstances!"

"I know. I know you didn't kill her."

"I *didn't* kill her. I would *never* have killed her. I should have gone over there the minute I got that bloody phone message."

"I don't think a few minutes would have made any difference."

Dylan shook his head and then kept shaking it. "I don't know what to do. I can't believe this is happening."

"You should hire a lawyer. That's the first thing."

"Yes." But Dylan didn't move. Maybe he'd already done so? He continued to huddle on the sofa looking very much like the victim of a hit and run.

Ellery squeezed his shoulder. "Maybe you won't be arrested. Maybe it won't come to that."

Dylan gave him another of those hollow-eyed stares. "There's no one else. They have no other suspects. Jack told me that last night. She wasn't on the island long enough to make enemies. He actually said that to me."

"She didn't have any friends either, so what does that tell you?"

"Jane Smith. They were friendly."

"Were they?"

"Perhaps? I don't know," Dylan said wearily. "I couldn't understand at first why no one, none of my friends seemed to like her." His red-rimmed gaze met Ellery's guilty one.

Ellery didn't bother to protest. He *hadn't* like September. He couldn't think of anyone who had. But he also couldn't think of anyone who'd disliked her enough to want to end her existence.

Dylan scrubbed his face with his hands. "When am I going to learn? I knew it was a mistake. I knew she was too young. I knew she was simply using me." He lowered his hands and gave Ellery a sad smile, "But I was using her, too."

A fair exchange of goods and services?

"Why did September move to Pirate's Cove? It doesn't seem like her kind of place."

"She said she was taking a break from acting to rest."

Ellery managed not to snort at the idea September had such a busy acting career she'd have needed to take a rest break. "Did she have family here? Did she have a history on the island?"

"I don't think so. She never said so."

"I feel like I never got to know her." That wasn't regret. Ellery had no interest in getting to know September. He was thinking aloud.

"I feel the same."

"Do you know if she *has* family? On the mainland, I mean."

"No. I realize now she was rather reticent about her past. That should have been the first red flag."

"Not necessarily." But in this case, yes. "What were her finances like?"

"Nonexistent." Dylan shrugged. "I was paying her rent. I didn't care about that. I was happy to help her out at first."

At first. Ellery suspected there was a *wealth*—no pun intended—of insight into Dylan and September's relationship concealed behind those two small words.

Dylan's head snapped up. He drew in a sharp breath and stared at the large arched window.

"What's wrong?" Ellery asked as Dylan jumped up from the sofa and went to the window.

"It's Jack!" Dylan gulped. His face had lost whatever color it had.

Ellery rose too. "Okay. Don't panic. It's not SWAT. Jack's not going to—"

"He's going to arrest me!"

Was he? Would Jack come on his own if he was planning to arrest Dylan? That wasn't protocol and Jack was quite the guy for protocol. But Jack was also kind and Dylan was a friend.

Ellery moved beside Dylan to gaze out the window.

Yep. It was Jack.

He had parked next to Ellery's VW. As Ellery and Dylan watched, the SUV's door opened and Jack got out. He gave Ellery's car a look that should have flattened all four of its tires, and then headed up the staggered granite pavers.

Dylan gave another of those backrow gasps and backed away from the window.

"Just...chill," Ellery ordered. "I'll answer the door. You—"

"No!"

"Dylan, he knows you're here. He knows *I'm* here. He's parked right next to my car."

"I'm not going to be treated like a common criminal."

"This is not useful. Seriously."

Dylan said wildly, "I'm not trying to be useful! Distract him. All I need is five minutes head start." He turned toward the door leading to the kitchen.

"*What*?" Ellery exclaimed. "Hell no, you're not going to flee. It's an island. Where would you flee to? Just...let me talk to Jack."

The doorbell rang, as loud and stagey as a theater bell board.

Dylan made a strangling sound and gulped out, "Therefore, send not to know. For whom the bell tolls, It tolls for thee!"

Ellery pointed to the sofa. "*Sit*."

Dylan collapsed onto the sofa and dropped his head in his hands.

A moment later, Ellery opened the front door to Jack. They stared at each other, and for a moment, it seemed like they were each looking at a stranger.

Ellery had almost forgotten how intimidating Jack could seem in his spic-and-span navy uniform with that aggressively shiny badge and all those bits of braid.

"Hey," Ellery said.

Jack, his green-blue gaze as bleak as the ocean in winter, said, "I really wish you weren't here."

Not the friendliest greeting. But then, the morning had started out with an argument, so there was already tension between them.

Ellery, always snappish when he was nervous, retorted, "I really wish *you* weren't here."

Jack's unsmiling mouth became a straight line. "You need to step outside."

"Oh, come *on*, Jack."

"I'm serious, Ellery. Step outside."

"Just give me a few minutes. I can try to calm him down. He's—"

Jack swore. He said tightly, "This is not up for discussion. You're interfering with an officer in the performance of his duties."

Ellery, unused to being addressed in that tone—let alone being sworn at, stammered, "A-are you kidding m-me? You're going to pull the *penal code card*? What are you doing, Jack? You're going to arrest one of our closest friends without even *trying* to investigate?"

That wasn't exactly what he'd meant to say. It didn't matter. The minute the words were out of his mouth, Ellery knew he'd made a serious mistake.

Jack's expression went from disbelieving to outraged to ice-cold control. His normally light, warm gaze went black and flat. He even seemed to grow a couple of inches. "*Excuse me*?"

"I don't understand your rush to—"

It was Carson the cop not Jack the boyfriend who broke in with a stony, "I *will not* tolerate any interference from you of all people. Do you understand?"

Not really. Especially not that harsh *you of all people*. What was that supposed to mean?

"*Seriously?*"

Jack's eyes flickered, but his stance did not soften.

"He's not guilty, Jack. If you could just give me a couple of days—"

"Are you freaking kidding me?" Jack did not raise his voice—if anything, it dropped an octave or two. "You think you're going to run a *counter-investigation* with my blessing?"

Ellery's voice also dropped. "With or without your bless-ing, I'm going to find out who killed September. Because it was *not* Dylan, and I think you kn—"

"Stand. Aside." There was no question Jack meant it.

Ellery stepped back from the doorway and Jack walked past him without a glance. Ellery followed in indignant si-lence. He felt shaky, his heart pounding as hard as if Jack had actually shoved him out of the way.

He followed Jack into the living room, where Dylan stood, as if at bay, in front of a shelf full of trophies and awards. Dylan didn't speak. He stared at Jack with an ex-pression reminiscent of Macbeth's at the sight of Banquo's ghost in the buffet line.

Jack, sounding only slightly less Robocop, began, "Dylan, I don't like this any more than you. I thought you might prefer to drive over to the jail with me. We won't need handcuffs if you—"

That was the point at which everything went sideways.

Maybe it was the word *handcuffs*. Maybe it was the word *jail*. Maybe it was everything everywhere all at once.

Whatever it was, Dylan sprang toward Jack, crying, "*I refuse to be taken prisoner!*"

Jack, abruptly sounding a lot less like Chief Carson and a lot more like himself, exclaimed, "Oh for—! Will you *please* not force me do this the hard way?"

It was doubtful Dylan heard him.

Fists up, he began to circle Jack, bobbing and weaving in a boxing style that had probably only ever existed in 1940s cartoons. Truth be told, with his tongue sticking out and hair standing up in tufts, he bore a worrying resemblance to Bugs Bunny.

"You won't take me alive, copper!" he panted.

"This can't be for real." Jack muttered. "I have to be dreaming."

Ellery brushed past him. "Dylan, listen to me. Don't resist arrest or it'll be harder for me to bail you out. Just go with him and I promise—"

"Are you kidding me?" Jack broke in. "You're going to spend the money you need to keep a roof over your head on his bail bond?"

Ellery tried to—well, he wasn't exactly sure. He was not trying to grab Dylan, he was trying to reassure him, soothe him, but Dylan seemed to view Ellery's approach as an attempt to subdue him. He knocked Ellery's hand away, bounced past him, and did a move resembling the Kazotsky Kick. In other circumstances, it would have been quite impressive for a man of his age—or a man of any age.

Jack was not impressed. "Dylan," he growled, "I'm not in the mood for this."

Dylan bounded up, bounced back and forth beneath Jack's nose—all the while pummeling the air with his fists.

Jack drew in a long breath and squared his shoulders. "I'm warning you—" He jerked his head back as Dylan's fist grazed his nose.

Ellery, recognizing that Jack had reached the end of his tether, pushed between them. "Okay. *Enough*."

Unfortunately, he miscalculated and managed to plant himself on the receiving end of the short, efficient jab Jack intended for Dylan. The punch caught Ellery on his chin, and he stumbled back, landing on his ass. There was a singing sound in his ears. For a few moments he saw stars.

A long time ago in a galaxy far, far away...

From an echoing distance, he heard Dylan's alarmed, "*Ellery!*" and Jack's horrified, "*Jesus Christ.*"

"Ouch," Ellery said. Which was an understatement. It wasn't the first time he'd been punched—accidents occasionally happened on set—but it was the first time he'd been punched by someone intending to get maximum results with minimum effort, and it hurt.

A lot.

The jolt of two large nerve clusters getting mashed together created a neurological overload that was both shocking and excruciatingly painful. The lights flickered and for a second or two his entire infrastructure teetered on total black out.

"Ellery?" Jack knelt beside him. "Can you hear me?" His hands, hands Ellery knew very well, were warm and gentle as he tipped Ellery's face up. "Let me see."

Ellery didn't try to respond. For one, he couldn't. For another, his instinct was to turn to Jack for comfort. So he kept his eyes shut and accepted Jack's help.

Jack's fingers lightly traced the throbbing junction of nerves behind Ellery's jaw. He swore softly and Ellery opened his eyes.

Jack's sun-streaked brown hair had fallen boyishly over his forehead. His eyes were wide with worry and remorse. "Are you okay?"

"I'm okay," Ellery said thickly. He'd bitten his tongue—hopefully not too badly—and he could feel it starting to swell. He wiggled his jaw and prayed that all of those years of braces and retainers had not been made irrelevant.

Jack made a small sound that fell somewhere between apology and asperity, and quit cradling Ellery's face. "Lucky for you, you've got a jaw like a donkey."

Perhaps not the ideal moment for home truths.

Ellery said ungraciously, "I only hope it hurt you as much as it hurt me." It came out more like, "Uh ohny hop ih hur yuh ah muh ah ih hur meh."

Jack said obliquely, "I'm sure it hurt me more."

"Ha!" Ellery retorted.

"It's my fault." Dylan sat on the sofa, head in hands. "Sorry, Ellery."

"Yep. It sure as hell is." Jack rose. "Of all the jackass moves. This is what I get for... I tried to give you the opportunity to come in on your own. *Now* we'll do it according to regulations. And we can add resisting arrest to the charges. Stand up, Dylan, and put your hands behind your back."

"Uh yuh fuuih kihhih meh?" Ellery protested.

Just for an instant, Jack's stern mask slipped. *"Really? I'm* the bad guy?"

Normally, Ellery would have had to concede that Jack sounded hurt, too hurt to hide it, but the last four minutes had left a negative impact—literally—and he preserved an unforgiving silence.

Dylan rose obediently. Jack snapped the cuffs on Dylan's wrists and proceeded to Mirandize him, which was surely adding insult to injury.

Jack said tersely, "Do you understand your rights as I've explained them to you?"

"How did I never realize what a complete and utter fascist you are." Dylan showed a flicker of his old spirit.

Jack sighed. "I'll take that as a yes. Ellery, do you need a ride to the med center?"

"Noh."

Jack hesitated. "Are you sure?"

Ellery glared at him.

Jack's face tightened. "Suit yourself then."

Ellery pushed up from the floor. He was still wobbly and he made an ungraceful transfer from carpet to nearest chair, all the while aware of Jack's troubled gaze.

"Will you lock up here?" Dylan asked Ellery. His voice wasn't quite steady.

Ellery nodded.

Jack opened his mouth, then closed it, and Ellery realized that Dylan's house and property would shortly be searched for evidence that he'd murdered September.

CHAPTER THIRTEEN

"**I**'ve already been told by Chief Carson not to discuss the St. Simmons case with you," Rob greeted Ellery when he arrived at the Buck Island Med Center.

In another lifetime, after getting punched in the face, Ellery would have spent the afternoon lying on his sofa with an ice pack, the TV remote control in hand. In this alternate reality, people, who should have known better, were relying on him for everything from keeping them out of prison to keeping them alive.

He was not feeling very well, but fear and panic were great energizers. So after generously dosing himself with Dylan's OTC painkillers and icing his jaw for a few minutes, he'd returned to action.

"Jack phoned you?" Ellery couldn't help that little note of outrage.

"No. Last night. At the crime scene." Rob's smile was wry. "Apparently, he knows you pretty well."

Apparently, Jack knew them both pretty well.

Rob added, "In any case, I'm not doing the autopsy, so it's not as if I could tell you much."

Ellery and Rob had grown close over the past months. Not as close as they would have been if Rob hadn't been romantically interested in Ellery. Rob played by the rules, but his desire for more was always there, and it occasionally put a strain on their friendship. That was because of Jack. Jack was well aware of Rob's feelings. He insisted he trusted Ellery, but he also admitted he was jealous.

And, honestly, Rob was just Ellery's type—in a world that didn't contain Jack Carson. So Ellery was always careful, always mindful he was not sending mixed messages.

He dropped into the chair across from Rob, leaning forward, and folding his arms on the desktop.

"Welll, you could *probably* tell me a few things that would be helpful. If you were so inclined."

Rob shook his head, but it seemed to Ellery that was not so much a *no* as resignation.

"How long had she been dead?"

Rob cocked his head, his green eyes studied Ellery quizzically, but he answered, "Not long. She was still warm and rigor hadn't set in."

Ellery mentally mined his store of mystery novel-based forensic knowledge. "Less than three hours?"

Rob nodded approvingly. "You're getting better at this. I'd say even less than that. Frankly, I think it's a very good thing you didn't arrive on scene any earlier."

"Yikes."

"Yeah. Speaking of dangerous run-ins, what happened to your jaw?"

Ellery grimaced. He was hoping the ice might have mitigated some of the swelling. At least he no longer sounded punch drunk. "I tried to break up a fight."

"Nora and Mr. Peabody going at it again?"

Ellery laughed and then winced.

"Let me take a look."

Robert rose, checked him out with brisk but kindly efficiency. "You'll want to use ice to control the swelling.

You're probably going to have a bruise for the next week or so."

"Good thing I don't have another photoshoot lined up."

Rob thought he was kidding. "Any loose teeth?"

"No. Thank God."

"You should probably stick to soft foods for the next few days. Would you like a script for the pain?"

"I've got stuff at home."

Rob retook his seat behind the desk. "The good news is your mother saw to it you drank your milk and ate your veggies."

"She did, yeah. Is there any doubt that September was killed by being hit with a hammer?"

"No. She died from blunt force trauma. Three blows, I'd say, and the first probably did her in. Someone was *very* angry when they struck her."

"Was she hit from behind?"

"Yes. I'd say she was carrying a tray of drinks from the kitchen into the living room when she was struck. The drinks tray, ice bucket, and cocktail glasses were on the floor of the living room."

"I couldn't see that from the doorway."

Robert raised his eyebrows, but added, "She was wearing a flowy white negligee. Her face was made up."

Ellery's heart sank. "She wasn't just *expecting* company; the company had arrived."

"That's the way it looked to me."

Makeup, sexy nightwear, and cocktails seemed to indicate a gentleman caller. Still, just because September had been expecting Dylan to show up, didn't mean someone else couldn't have arrived first.

It didn't look good though. Ellery had to admit that.

"It would have been a crime of impulse though, right? Jack said it appeared her killer had grabbed the hammer September was using to break up a block of ice."

Rob was silent, listening to the overhead speakers paging Dr. Lippencott. He returned his attention to Ellery. "Are you asking or telling?"

"Both, I guess."

"It could have happened that way, yes. There was a bloody hammer on the kitchen table, where the, er, perp, I guess you'd call him, left it on his way out. And there was a partially melted block of ice in the sink, which also helps with your timeline."

"Right." Ellery said slowly, "How strong do you have to be to kill someone with a hammer?"

"Provided you're not afraid to hit and hit hard, it's a good weapon. It wouldn't be about strength so much as aggression and confidence. You have to get close to use a hammer. There isn't any striking from a safe distance. You have to rely on surprise or overwhelming force."

Ellery nodded, considering. Dylan was physically fit and confident in his physicality. No question he could have bashed September's head in, but *would* he have bashed her head in? It was a gruesome thought, but if Dylan was angry enough to commit murder, Ellery could more easily picture him strangling September than hitting her over the head with a blunt instrument.

Did that make sense?

For Dylan to attack a woman, he'd have to be so completely out of control, so beside himself—

Oh. That was it. That was the point.

If Dylan was *that* enraged, it would be apparent to whoever was enraging him. And how likely was it that that person would then blithely turn their back on him and toddle off with a tray full of cocktail fixings?

Not likely at all, in Ellery's opinion.

Especially given that September had to know Dylan well enough to recognize when he was upset. Yes, September had seemed on the oblivious side. But Dylan wasn't the seethe-in-silence type. When Dylan was riled, everyone around him knew it.

"Are you having a break-through?" Rob inquired.

"Hm? More like a breakdown."

Rob laughed. "Maybe you should learn to say no. To someone besides me, I mean."

And there it was. Rob was kidding, but not entirely. This was why Jack was not enthusiastic about their friendship.

Ellery said, "A woman could have killed September."

"Do you suspect a woman of killing her?"

"No. I don't have any suspects so far."

"She'd only been on the island a month or two, right?"

"Since July."

Rob said comfortingly, "Some people make enemies faster than others. It's important to remember that these changes happen at different times for everyone."

Ellery laughed—and then winced. Robert's green eyes got a mischievous twinkle.

He said casually, "Since Chief Carson's going to be busy with his murder case, would you like to go to the concert at Loon Landing tonight?"

Ellery said caustically, "Chief Carson's already made his arrest, so I don't know if he'll be working much overtime."

Rob looked startled. "Who'd he arrest?"

That brought Ellery up short. He hadn't intended to share any information not available to the public. But then again, it's not as though Dylan's arrest could be kept secret.

"Dylan Carter."

"*Dylan Carter?*" Rob looked astounded. "No way."

"Right?" Ellery was gratified at Rob's instant rejection of Dylan's guilt.

"I mean, you can never tell, but..."

"You can tell in this case," Ellery said shortly.

Robert considered him. He made a soft, "*Ah.*"

Ellery grimaced. He was depressed by the reminder that he and Jack were on the outs. He rose. "I should get going. Can I call you about tonight?"

"You can call me anytime," Robert assured him.

* * * * *

When Ellery arrived at the Crow's Nest a short time later, he fully expected to find the Silver Sleuths in residence, so it was a jolt to walk into the bookshop and find it as empty and quiet as a...bookshop.

Kingston was reshelving books and Nora stood at the sales desk, sorting through a battered cardboard box full of old paperbacks.

At the jangle of the doorbell, Watson dropped his chew toy and came rocketing up the aisle to loudly relate the sweet sorrow of their parting.

"I know. But I'm here now." Ellery took a moment to reassure his little pal that the feelings were mutual.

Nora observed their reunion, and when she could get a word in, said, "There you are, dearie. We were starting to worry. How did the photoshoot go?"

That crazy photoshoot seemed like something that had happened months ago.

"Fine. Where is everybody?" Ellery glanced around the empty bookshop.

Nora and Kingston, who had joined her at the counter, exchanged glances.

"Probably at Loon Landing, don't you think?" Nora said. "It's the first full day of the festival."

"No, I mean the Silver Sleuths. Where are they?"

"Oh." Nora looked at Kingston.

"*Oh*?" Ellery looked from Nora to Kingston. "What does that tone of *oh* mean? You know Dylan was arrested, right?"

Kingston said, "Er, yes."

Ellery did a doubletake. "Is there a man with a gun hiding in my office? What's going on with you two?"

In seeming digression, Nora said, "Chief Carson phoned twice."

"Oh, did he?" Ellery said darkly.

Nora glanced at Kingston again and said, "He was concerned that you weren't experiencing any aftereffects after he..." She cleared her throat delicately. "Punched you."

"He told you he punched me?"

Nora and Kingston nodded solemnly.

Ellery cautiously wiggled his jaw. "That wasn't Jack's fault. Dylan panicked at the idea of being arrested, and I stupidly jumped between them."

"All the same, I think Chief Carson feels very badly."

"Ya think?" Ellery was remembering that *lucky for you, you've got a jaw like a donkey* crack. He said shortly, "Well, he should. But not about me. He should feel bad about arresting Dylan."

"I don't think he feels very good about it," Kingston offered. "I suspect he didn't feel he had a choice."

"After all, there's a lot of circumstantial evidence," Nora said.

Ellery automatically put a hand to the swelling on his jaw. "Are you telling me, *you* both think Dylan is guilty?"

"Certainly not!" Nora said.

Kingston echoed, "Never!"

"Good, because I'm not going to stand by and let Dylan go to prison for a crime *I* know he didn't commit."

Nora's eyes lit with excitement. "*Excellent*! We were hoping you'd feel that way."

"I'm glad to hear it. I might need some...." He caught himself before he actually said the fatal word *backup,* changing it for, "Input."

"Of course! You know you can count on us," Nora assured him.

Ellery absently picked up a tattered paperback from the box on the desk, studied the image of a sinister-looking man opening a drawer with a skull. *Lady, That's My Skull* read the title. He returned the book to the box. "I still can't believe that less than twenty-four hours into the investigation, Jack thought he had enough evidence to arrest Dylan."

Nora made a noncommittal, "*Mm.*"

Kingston coughed. "I believe there are pressures on Chief Carson that forced his hand."

Ellery shook his head. "I don't know that that's true. His mind seemed made up last night."

Nora *tsk-tsked*, but then, catching Kingston's eye, she said, "I know it would bother Chief Carson very much to think you believed he would arrest Mr. Carter without sufficient cause or evidence."

"Well, I do believe it," Ellery said shortly. "I think Jack rushed to judgement on this. Which I can't understand because it isn't even like him. And Dylan's a friend. Which makes it worse."

Kingston caught Nora's eye. Nora said, "Chief Carson takes his responsibilities very seriously."

"You don't have to tell me!"

Nora sighed and tried again. "Perhaps Chief Carson is reacting so, er, decisively because he's... sensitive to the criticism he received when he refused to be pressured into arresting you for Brandon Abbott's murder."

Ellery frowned. "Okay, but I was innocent. He was right not to arrest me."

"Perhaps he was more convinced of your innocence than Mr. Carter's," Kingston offered.

"Perhaps. In which case he's wrong. About Dylan being guilty, I mean. Anyway, I need to find out when Dylan's bail bond hearing—" Ellery started toward his office.

"Mr. Carter's already out on bail," Nora interrupted.

Ellery stopped in his tracks, turning to face them. "What? How? He was only just arrested."

"Janet Maples bailed him out."

"*Janet?*" That was a surprise, but also a huge relief. It wasn't that Ellery had been eager to spend his roof money on Dylan's bond. He had assumed there was no alternative.

"From what we understand, he'll be staying with her for the time being."

"That's great. I had no idea things were moving so quickly." And in the right direction, for once.

Nora said, "Janet used to work for the police department. That was before your time, of course. I suspect Chief Carson might have given her a heads-up."

Ellery considered that possibility. That move was certainly more like the Jack he knew than the Jack who'd shown up to arrest Dylan that morning. He regarded Nora and Kingston's unusually serious expressions, replayed the conversation of the last few minutes—and reviewed what felt a bit like the public relations efforts of his trusted associates.

"I get it." Ellery rejoined Nora behind the sales desk. "You think I'm being unfair to Jack. But you weren't there this morning. He was *not* pleasant. Let me put it that way. And that was *before* I got hit in the face."

Kington removed his spectacles and wiped them. "Perhaps Chief Carson was a little flustered to find you there?"

"Jack? *Flustered*? No way."

Nora said, "Chief Carson thinks the world of you, dearie. He knows how you'd view what must have seemed necessary action on his part. Feeling like a-a stormtrooper couldn't have been very nice for him."

Ellery snorted.

Kingston said, "Indeed not. I expect it made him defensive and maybe a bit angry to find himself in such a position. He was probably in a hurry to put an end to an embarrassing situation."

This was an angle Ellery had not considered—he was not entirely convinced by Nora and Kingston's reasoning—but Jack had definitely seemed off balance that morning.

He idly picked up another paperback. *Trigger Mortis* proclaimed the title.

"Where did these come from?"

"Imelda dropped them off yesterday evening. It's a nice haul."

Ellery nodded absently. Imelda, who worked at the veterinary office, was one of their best customers. He met Nora's gaze and made a face. "Okay. I'll give Jack a call. Meanwhile, maybe you should summon the troops."

Nora did not go so far as to high five Kingston, but Ellery suspected she would have if he hadn't been watching.

He went into his office and phoned Jack's cell, but Jack did not pick up. That was disappointing, but also partly a relief. He was still shocked that Jack, *his* Jack, could be as heartless and cold as he'd seemed that morning. Getting clocked hadn't hurt a fraction as much as Jack saying, *you're interfering with an officer in the performance of his duties.* That (literal) pulling of rank felt unfair, unjustified on several levels.

At the same time, he acknowledged his presence at Dylan's had definitely not helped matters. In fact, if he'd realized Jack was going to make an arrest, he'd have steered clear.

As it was, they found themselves in new and threatening territory. Where they went from here, Ellery was unsure.

CHAPTER FOURTEEN

"First, we have to look at motive," Nora was saying as she doled out neatly typed pages to the circle of sleuths gathered in the Crow's Nest open area.

"For which case?" Stanley Starling inquired.

"*Dear* Mr. Carter *has* to take precedence." Edna glanced around the circle. "We're all in agreement surely?"

The others murmured assent, flipping dossier pages back and forth. Ellery, counting out the cash drawer, hoped he hadn't made yet another miscalculation in calling for this emergency meeting at the clubhouse.

"Very well," Hermione said briskly. "What have we got on our victim?"

Once again there was much scraping and flapping of papers, before Nora admitted, "Not much, I'm afraid."

"There's an understatement," Stanley remarked.

Nora sniffed. "I'm not a magician. I have to have something to work with."

"Her driver's license?" Hermione questioned. "That's the only documentation we have on Ms. St. Simmons?"

Mrs. Ferris gasped. "WITSEC!" she exclaimed. "It explains everything."

"Well, not *everything*, dear," Nora said.

Stanley said, "It doesn't explain what WITSEC is, for one thing."

Kingston supplied, "United States Federal Witness Protection Program."

Stanley made a noise of dismissal, which was Ellery's reaction, too.

"No, but let's consider," Mrs. Ferris insisted. "It explains why the woman seems to have no history. It explains why someone like her would come to our remote island in the first place."

"We're not *that* remote," Hermione objected.

Mrs. Ferris was undeterred. "This wasn't her sort of place. She wasn't our sort of person. She didn't fit in at all. She wasn't happy here and she made no bones about showing it. *And,* mostly importantly, being a witness for the government explains why, despite the fact that there's no motive for and no suspect in her death, she was murdered."

As none of the others seemed to know how to answer that, Ellery said, "Well, unfortunately, there is a suspect. What if we tried to build the case against Dylan as if we were the police? Once we understand why they think he's the only one who could have done this, we can figure out how to knock their case to pieces."

"We'll play devil's advocate," Nora said. "Yes! That's very good."

"It's easy enough to understand why the police have settled on Mr. Carter," Mrs. Ferris said. "The police believe it's a lust murder."

"*Whaaa*?" objected Stanley. "What now?"

"A. LUST. MURDER," Mrs. Ferris enunciated clearly.

Ellery, who'd paused to take a sip of bottled water, choked and began to cough.

"I'm not hard of hearing, woman. I heard you the first time. I just want to know what the heck you're smoking."

Nora, who had hopped up to deliver a couple of hard, swift blows to Ellery's back, said with just a hint of impatience, "I don't believe that's the angle the police are working, dear."

Mrs. Ferris said defensively, "It's the only thing that makes sense to *me*."

Ellery stopped coughing and croaked, "*Nobody* thinks Dylan is a lust murderer!"

"I'm not saying he *is*. I'm saying that's the direction the police investigation will surely take."

Kingston said, "It's certainly a theory. However, perhaps we should start with the possible motives for removing Ms. St. Simmons."

"In a lust murder—"

"Yes, yes," Kingston said hastily. "However, let's consider *other* possible motives. Did Ms. St. Simmons possess knowledge that was dangerous to someone else?"

"There's plenty of that on this island," Ellery said darkly, taking his chair within the circle. Watson came to him, placing his fat puppy paws on Ellery's knees, and Ellery lifted him up. "Right?" he asked Watson.

Watson wagged his tail.

"What did you do to your face, Ellery?" Hermione asked suddenly. "You're getting quite a bruise on your jaw."

Seven pairs of eyes—eight, counting Watson—were suddenly trained on him like laser sights. "Oh, I..."

"Someone punched him," Stanley remarked. "Noticed it the minute I walked in. It's a dangerous business asking questions. A lot of people don't like it."

Ellery sighed. "Could we *please* just concentrate..."

"Yes," Nora said briskly. "Now. It's possible Ms. St. Simmons arrived in Pirate's Cove already in possession of knowledge dangerous to someone on the island. However, I think it's unlikely she gained any such knowledge here. For one thing, she doesn't seem to have had any close friends or confidantes."

"She had Mr. Carter," Mrs. Ferris said.

"Yes, but Mr. Carter has had many, *many* romantic liaisons over the years," Nora pointed out. "It's difficult to believe he confided something worth committing murder over to Ms. St. Simmons but not to anyone else."

"If he was going to confide in any woman it would be Janet Maples," Stanley opined.

Nora concurred.

Edna's tone was reflective. "She was awfully chummy with Jane for a while. The St. Simmons woman, I mean."

"That's true," Hermione said. "I was surprised, to be honest. They didn't seem to have much in common."

"Someone needs to speak to Jane," Nora informed Ellery.

"You mean me? Okay. I'll try." After his encounter with Jane earlier that day, he wasn't sure how far he'd get. But he was curious as to what she'd been doing skulking outside Lara's suite at the Seacrest Inn.

Kingston asked, "Do we know if she left a will?"

Mrs. Ferris gave another of those unnerving gasps. "Perhaps she left something in a safety deposit box!"

"Like what, dear?" Nora inquired with slightly strained patience.

"Her will. *Or* the information for which someone was willing to kill her."

"We don't yet know that either of those things exist."

"Perhaps Jane will know."

"I'll ask," Ellery put in. "But I know she—September, that is—was hard up financially. Dylan was paying her rent and probably more."

"Jane's hard up, too," Hermione remarked.

"No wonder she sunk her claws so deep into him," Stanley said. "A man of Carter's age and experience should have known better."

"Really, Stanley? *Sunk her claws*?" Hermione repeated.

"Don't *Stanley* me. The woman was a gold-digger. Anyone could see it."

Ellery's head was starting to ache. He pinched the bridge of his nose. "Maybe she was in someone's way?"

"Janet's!" Mrs. Ferris said.

Ellery opened his mouth, but really, was that any sillier than any of the other suggestions posed so far? The fact of the matter was, he couldn't see a whole lot of motive for anyone needing to get September out of the way by any means necessary.

He said, "Okay, maybe there wasn't a motive as we understand motive."

"What does that mean?" Stanley asked the room at large. "Young feller's got concussion!"

"I mean, maybe it was a crime of passion." Ellery caught Mrs. Ferris's eye and said quickly, "Not *that* kind of passion. Not lust. I mean heat-of-the-moment type passion. Because her murder wasn't premeditated. We know that for a fact. September's murderer used a weapon of opportunity."

"The hammer." Edna shivered.

"Exactly. Her killer didn't go there planning to kill her."

Stanley said, "Could have planned to strangle her. Decided the hammer was easier. It takes a lot of strength to throttle someone." He held his hands out and flexed them menacingly.

Edna and Hermione exchanged disapproving looks.

Ellery surreptitiously checked his phone. No messages from Jack. No messages from anyone.

He wanted to get over to Loon Landing to talk to Arti Rathbone before the Fish and Chippies went on. He wanted to be there when Lara performed, not least because that would doubtlessly be the best time to catch Jane. She would surely want to see Lara perform "Angel Beneath the Waves." Even Ellery was curious to see how the final version of the song turned out.

He'd been hoping this summoning of the troops would prove more useful than it had so far. Since Jane's departure, Mrs. Ferris had begun to take a much more dynamic role in the group, with, he couldn't help feeling, mixed results. Certainly, Mrs. Ferris brought a...a unique point of view to the discussions, but Ellery wasn't convinced her input was entirely helpful.

In fact, he was thinking he should probably give this up as a lost cause and get over to the festival grounds ASAP.

Nora, who didn't miss much, seemed to pick up on his mood. She said briskly, "Let me do some additional fact finding. We can regroup tomorrow. Turning our attention to the question of who might want Lara Fairplay out of the way..."

There were murmurs of agreement and hasty flipping of pages. Ellery didn't think he imagined that air of relief from the others.

"Money. Sex. Power." That, naturally, was Mrs. Ferris.

"I think we can rule out power." Ellery said. "Lara's struggling to make a comeback. I don't think she's posing a threat to anyone musically or personally."

"Revenge," Stanley said. "The family of the woman she killed isn't satisfied with eleven years in prison. Neither would I be."

"If you'll look at your dossiers," Nora advised with strained patience. "I've covered this angle extensively."

Ellery, along with the others, scanned Nora's notes while Nora gave them a verbal overview. "It seems the stories that were carried in the media didn't give a completely accurate picture of the circumstances of Shumway's death. The poor woman had been in and out—sadly more out than in—of psychiatric treatment for most of her adult life. Her parents are deceased. Her siblings disowned her."

"Why?" Ellery asked.

"Dawn claimed she'd been robbed of her share of the money and property her parents left to be divided among her and her siblings. According to the family, no amount of paperwork or proof could otherwise convince her. Eventually, she began threatening her nieces and nephews, whereupon her family cut all ties with her."

"Did none of that come out in the trial?"

"It was ruled inadmissible, according to the article I read. The family professed sadness but not surprise at her death."

Ellery nodded, returned to reading. The name **James Sutherland** popped out from the lines of text.

At the same moment, Hermione asked, "James Sutherland. Was that the boy who won the music scholarship but..."

"Killed himself by mixing a bottle of vodka with a bottle of pills? Yes," Nora said.

"Terrible," Kingston murmured, and the others agreed.

"Perhaps it *wasn't* suicide?" Mrs. Ferris suggested.

"As a matter of fact, we don't know that it was," Nora answered. "James didn't leave a note and his death was ultimately ruled accidental."

Ellery repeated, "*Accidental*?"

"Yes. But that may have been out of consideration for the family. It seems the consensus of his friends was that he'd been severely depressed."

"I remember something about this," Stanley said. "It was over a girl, right? That was the rumor."

Nora said, "There was never any official mention of a girl."

"You mean, no girl was named?" Stanley asked.

"Correct."

"But *we* know who the girl was." Stanley looked at Ellery.

Ellery said, "Lara suggested that James might be somebody on the island with a grudge against her. She obviously doesn't know he's dead."

"What about his family? What about his friends?" Hermione objected. "They might feel they have reason to hold a grudge."

"They might," Ellery said. "But if you're angry enough to kill someone, do you wait more than twenty years to do it?"

"This is the first time Lara's returned to the island," Edna pointed out. "The first time they had the opportunity."

Nora said briskly, "The family moved from the island after James died. I don't believe that could be a factor."

"After all, Lara *hasn't* been killed," Kingston said thoughtfully. "She's had two close calls that might or might not be accidents. She's either very lucky *or* it's possible she had forewarning."

"A publicity stunt!" For once Mrs. Ferris echoed the thoughts of everyone else.

She didn't even miss a beat.

Ellery considered Jocasta's earlier comment. He considered the likelihood of being concerned enough to hire someone to find out the source of death threats, yet not keep a single copy of those death threats.

"I think it's possible," he admitted. "Jocasta Fairplay mentioned the hoped-for comeback hasn't been a blazing success so far. They're not getting the media coverage they expected. Maybe the idea is to give the media something to write about?"

It would also explain not hiring real bodyguards. Not to mention recruiting a local bookseller versus employing a private eye to find out who was sending death threats.

He said, "Even if someone *is* sending threats, it doesn't mean they intend to act on them. The threats themselves might be the revenge." He was thinking of Arti Rathbone, who had been friends with James, might know some of the factors that caused him to take his life, and *was* still on the island.

"True," Kingston said. "That's a good point."

Nora said, "I can't help thinking that sending a warning to someone you intend to kill is merely making your own life more difficult."

Ellery grinned, "So you wouldn't send ominous threats to your intended victim, Nora?"

"Indeed no. I would bide my time until the right moment and then...KAPOW!!!"

Everyone jumped. Watson, who had been slumbering peacefully on Ellery's lap, leaped to the floor and began barking.

Arf! Arf! Arf!

Sure, Watson was barking at the front door, rather than at the culprit, but he had the right idea.

"Ohh. Kay." Ellery shuffled his papers together and rose. "Thank you all. This has been very helpful. It's getting late. I think I'd better get over to Loon Landing."

"What time is it?" exclaimed Mrs. Ferris. "Mr. Ferris will be expecting his dinner."

The others rose too and began the inevitable dropping of papers and spectacles and phones as they reached for coats and sweaters and purses.

Nora called, "Stanley, don't you sneak out of here. You need to help Kingston put these chairs back in the junk room."

"*Or* you could stack them in my *office*," Ellery said pointedly.

Stanley, who had been slinking toward the front door, turned with an innocent look. "Of course! Of course!"

Ellery spotted Kingston attempting to capture Watson, who seemed to believe they were playing a delightful game of tag.

"Watson," Ellery called sternly.

Watson looked around as though convinced that voice must surely be coming from the Great Beyond, and darted off toward Ellery's office, narrowly missing tripping Mr. Starling.

"Don't worry, I'll put him in his crate," Kingston assured Ellery, waving off Ellery's thanks. He added, "Do be careful over there, Ellery. I can't help feeling there's something sinister at work here. Some connection we keep overlooking."

CHAPTER FIFTEEN

Ellery was hoping to run into Jack.

With PICO PD handling so much of Sing the Plank's security, it made sense that Jack would be on site for much of Saturday night. Typically, Jack would have let Ellery know his plans—typically, Ellery would have let Jack know *his* plans. The prolonged radio silence was not encouraging, and Ellery wished that he'd left a message when he'd phoned Jack earlier.

By that point, the events of the morning felt surreal.

Ellery still couldn't understand why Jack had taken the action he had, but he was more than willing to hear what Jack had to say—and to accept responsibility for his own part in the unfortunate unfolding of events. He wasn't sure he agreed with Nora's and Kingston's armchair analysis of Jack's state of mind. He knew Jack cared for him, but he didn't kid himself that Jack placed any great importance on his opinions, especially when it came to how Jack did his job.

Jack's withdrawal triggered Ellery's old insecurity where Jack was concerned. He could all too easily envision Jack deciding Ellery was not the right boyfriend for Pirate's Cove's chief of police. That, between the amateur sleuthing and *interfering with an officer in the performance of his duties*, Ellery was proving himself to be a liability.

Partly, he could thank Todd for instilling in him that in-
stinctive fear that if he was not an actual asset in his partner's life, he was a liability. But partly, he hadn't forgotten
Jack's reluctance to get involved in the first place. Jack had
explained all that. He had reassured Ellery. It wasn't Jack's
fault that Ellery remained a little uncertain about Jack's level of commitment. But it wasn't entirely unreasonable either, especially when Jack had flat out said he wasn't ready
to make any commitments.

Anyway, Ellery was hoping he might casually run into
Jack, and then maybe, hopefully, they would each see that
the other was ready for a truce.

The cove at Loon Landing was significantly more crowded than the previous night, so that was good news. A line
led all the way from inside the boathouse to the end of the
dock, but the smaller stages had audiences, too. People wandered around with food and drink, and everyone seemed to
be having a good time.

Eventually, Ellery spotted Jack by a booth where souvenir T-shirts were being sold. He started to make his way
over, but realized it was maybe not the best time. Jack
seemed to be reading the riot act to a young female officer
who looked close to tears.

Ellery reversed mid-step at the exact same moment Jack
happened to glance in his direction. They locked eyes.

Could you feel the weight of someone's gaze in your
heart? Because that long, level look—

"Ouch!" someone said from behind Ellery.

Ellery started, turned to find Rob grimacing. "Rob! Was
that your *foot*? I thought you were tree stump."

"I've noticed." Rob was kidding, but it was a rueful kind
of kidding.

Ellery didn't get it for a moment, then he remembered. He gasped. "Oh my God. I was supposed to phone about this evening."

Rob laughed, but it wasn't his usual laugh. "That's okay."

"Rob, I'm so sorry."

"No worries. You're on the case. I know." Rob's mockery seemed to be directed more at himself than Ellery, but Ellery still winced.

"There's no excuse. I really am sorry."

"No, come on," Robert said. "It's not a big deal. I'm glad I ran into you—or you ran into me. I was hoping for a chance to say goodbye."

"*Goodbye*?" Ellery repeated. "Where are you going?"

Rob's usually direct gaze seemed to avoid his own. "I'm taking some time off. Flying home to Oregon."

Home to Oregon? Since when was Oregon home? Granted, Rob was from Oregon. His family was still there.

"This is kind of sudden, isn't it?"

Robert made a noncommittal sound. "Not really. I've been toying with the idea for a while. I have some thinking to do."

Ellery's brows drew together. "You can't think here?"

Robert smiled faintly. "Not really. No. I think I need a complete break."

That sounded serious. Seriously disappointing, for sure. Ellery enjoyed Robert's friendship. It was nice having someone to do things with when Jack wasn't around, which was more often than Ellery liked. That was the downside of dating a cop. It was probably worse when that cop was the chief of police.

"I'll miss you," he admitted.

Rob's smile was wry. "I'm thinking not that much."

Ellery groaned. "Rob, I'm sorry about forgetting to call. It's just been a crazy day."

One of the craziest days of his life.

"No. Really. I'm teasing you. I know you're under pressure. Dylan Carter's a good friend. Of course you've got to do everything you can to help him."

"You're a friend too, though, and I feel like I've let you down."

"No." Rob spoke firmly. "This isn't about you. Except tangentially. It just finally dawned on me that it's not going to be as easy to build a life here as I'd imagined."

"Oh." Ellery tried to read Rob's face in the twilight.

"Originally, that wasn't a high priority, but it's become more so in recent months."

"I...see."

Rob's mouth curved faintly. "I'm sure you do."

Yes, Ellery understood what Rob was saying, and he was sorry. Rob was lonely and the dating opportunities for a gay man in Pirate's Cove were limited.

In fact, for the first couple of months after his arrival, Ellery had wondered if he was the only LGBTQIA person on the entire island. It turned out Robert and Jack had both been there the whole time, so it was possible Robert's perfect match was hiding in plain sight, too. But he could also understand why Rob might feel it was time for a more proactive approach.

"How long do you think you'll be gone?"

"A month. Maybe more."

"That's...a long time." It sounded alarmingly permanent. "You're taking a leave of absence from the Med Center?"

"I am. Yeah."

Ellery said truthfully, "Here I was, thinking the week couldn't get any worse."

Rob grinned, squeezed Ellery's shoulder. "You're a very sweet guy, Mr. Page."

The timing was, as usual, terrible, but he felt he owed it to Rob to ask, "Did you want to see if we can get seats for one of the concerts?"

Rob moved his head in negation. "I'm headed home." His hand tightened on Ellery's shoulder and he drew him in for a quick, light kiss. "Goodbye, Ellery."

Ellery said reluctantly, "Bye, Rob..."

Robert turned and walked away.

Unsurprisingly, Jack was nowhere in sight when Ellery looked for him.

Well, Jack's expression had not exactly been welcoming even before Ellery bumped into Rob, so after that kiss goodbye (which Jack might or might not have seen) it was probably wiser to postpone any potential reunion to such time as there were no witnesses. Just in case Jack felt like punching him again.

HE WAS KIDDING.

But as it was unlikely Jack would ever find the humor in the events of that morning, Ellery would keep that joke to himself.

He headed into the boathouse, asked for Dylan, and was told Dylan was not planning to attend the evening's concerts.

That was not completely unexpected, though it would have been helpful to speak to Dylan about the accident with the trapdoor the previous evening—not to mention a few other topics of interest.

Instead, he settled for making his way backstage to see if he could find Arti Rathbone.

He arrived just in time to catch the Fish and Chippies packing up their gear.

Their set had gone well and they were in great spirits, talking and joking around. Ellery was greeted mostly with curiosity. David Fish looked less than enthusiastic to see him. He turned to have a quiet word with a slender woman with black hair and startlingly blue eyes.

Arti Rathbone glanced around, examined Ellery, and offered a cool smile.

Ellery asked if it might be possible to have a word. Fish said at once, "I'll go with you, Arti."

Arti gave Fish an amused look. "He's not the police, David, and even if he was, I don't have anything to hide."

Fish said to Ellery, "Our next set is in half an hour."

"Okay. I'll keep that in mind."

Arti rolled her eyes, hefted her accordion case, gave Ellery's shoulder a not-unfriendly thump, and said, "Lead on, Macduff." She strongly reminded Ellery of the girls he'd known at Tisch.

Ellery led the way along the corridor of dressing rooms, throwing back, "College theater major?"

Arti gave a short laugh. "Yep."

He immediately liked her.

Ellery pushed open the emergency exit side door and they stepped into the cool night. It was dark now. No stars shone overhead. The air was damp and heavy. It felt like rain. Dew sparkled in the grass. A symphony of crickets competed with the slosh of tide hitting the boathouse pilings and the music drifting from the outdoor stages. In the distance, ghost lights flickered over the marsh.

There was an empty folding chair sitting a few yards away, and Ellery snagged it, delivered it to Arti. Arti lowered her accordion case to the grass and sat down. "Thanks." Green glittered in her hair. Her eyes were made up to look like mermaid eyes.

Arti tilted her face up, considering him. "Let me save us both some time. I have no idea who's sending Lara threatening letters."

Ellery was unsurprised to realize Fish had filled Arti in on the threats Lara had received. He'd sort of figured that would happen, based on Fish's defensiveness when asked about Arti.

"You don't have any hard feelings toward Lara?"

Arti seemed to consider. "Not really. Not now. At the time? Sure."

"Lara told me about the record deal with White Wine Records," Ellery said. "She also said she thought it was unlikely you and James were sending those letters."

"That was gracious of her." Arti's tone was sardonic. She gazed out at the marsh lights, sighed, said softly, "Jamie."

This was the part of amateur sleuthing Ellery had no aptitude for. No heart for, to be honest. Arti sounded sad, and he was not built to jump on someone's emotional vulnerabilities, let alone exploit them. He didn't know what to say, so he said nothing.

After a few seconds, Arti looked up and gave a funny laugh. "Was that it?"

"I'm not sure. Do you know anything that could be useful?"

She did a doubletake, and her laughter sounded more natural that time. "Are you serious? The festival committee is *paying* you for this?"

Ellery spread his hands.

"Oh my God." She wiped her eyes on the back of her hand. "What a great gig."

"Do you think Jamie took his own life?" Ellery asked.

Arti stopped laughing. "Yeah. I do. Unfortunately."

"Because of Lara?"

In the gloom, he could just about make out her frown. "At the time, I did. But looking back... Obviously, he had emotional problems. I don't know why no one saw it. None of us recognized it. We just thought he was too sensitive. Took everything too seriously." She added, "It's not like Lara led him on. To be honest, she was probably one of the few people who didn't tiptoe around Jamie's feelings."

"You don't think these threats could have anything to do with what happened to James?"

"No way. Twenty—more than twenty—years later? Besides, they weren't in a relationship. Nobody, including James, thought they were. On top of that, White Wine dumped her a year into her contract. Which, I admit, I was pretty happy about at the time."

Arti had a point. Postponing your revenge for twenty years was taking procrastination to a whole new level. And, to continue pulling at that thread, why *bother* when Lara's life was already a train wreck?

"Can you think of anyone else on the island who might wish Lara harm?"

"On Buck Island? No. I seriously doubt anyone besides me even remembers her from those days."

"Do you think any of the other bands or musicians are so angry about Lara being brought in—"

Arti cut him off. "I know where you're going with this. No. I don't. David told me what Lara was being paid, and I admit, I was sort of outraged on his behalf. But I never said a word about it to anyone. David spoke to me in confidence. And he only told me because we're...together. Unofficially."

"Gotcha," Ellery said.

"It's not like he went around blabbing it to everyone."

"I understand."

"If someone *does* mean harm to Lara, I'm guessing it's from within her own inner circle."

Ellery said, "It's not a very large circle these days."

Arti said tartly, "Yeah, well I don't mean Joey."

Arti meant Neilson. The husband was always the default. Just like the boyfriend was always the default. If it wasn't true in Dylan's case, it might not be true in Neilson's case. Ellery didn't want his personal bias to blind him.

"Elon stuck with her when she went to prison."

"Did he?"

"He didn't divorce her. He waited eleven years for her. He's here now trying to help her rebuild her career."

"Because it's in his best interests." Art was scornful. "Don't kid yourself. Who else would hire him?"

Ellery said curiously, "Do you know Elon? Have you had dealings with him?"

"I don't have to be a snake charmer to know a snake when I see it."

Ellery started to answer. Arti stopped him. "Listen."

He listened, and in the lull between water and music he could hear a haunting, far-off wail.

"That's a loon." Arti said.

"That's kind of eerie." Beautiful, but definitely eerie.

"You should hear them laughing. It makes the hair stand up on your head."

They listened to the fluting calls of the loon for another second or two until its song faded into silence.

Ellery asked curiously, "How do you know Neilson Elon's a snake?"

Arti said, "I may not be earning my living from my music, but I still keep up with industry news. And industry gossip. And I still occasionally listen to Lara's music. You know her big hit single, 'Fool Me, Fool You'?"

"I've heard it."

"I guarantee you, it's about *him*. Neilson Elon. Next time you hear it, listen closely to the lyrics. It's about a woman who realizes her conman boyfriend is conning her along with everyone else, and sets out to pay him back in kind."

Ellery said slowly, "You think Lara is faking death threats to somehow set up her husband? What would the endgame be? To frame him for attempted murder?"

Arti's smile was a glimmer in the darkness. "I don't know. But if anyone could pull that off, it's Lara."

CHAPTER SIXTEEN

After Arti set off, lugging her accordion case, to meet her bandmates at Stage 3, Ellery returned to the boathouse, opened the side door, and found himself face-to-face with Jane Smith.

They startled each other, both jumping guiltily.

"*Ellery!*" Jane squeaked. "You frightened me." She peered more closely. "What happened to your face?"

"It's a long story. What are you—"

She wasn't listening. Not to him. Her head turned and he realized she was trying to hear the performance happening overhead.

> *Bravest of angels, return thee to me,*
> *From under the waves and over the sea,*
> *Gone is my peace, my heart aches with woe*
> *The dearest of men lies sleeping below.*

He had heard a bit of the song during the soundcheck, and had not been impressed. But this was different. It wasn't about the lyrics or the melody so much as the power and authenticity of Lara's voice. Ellery wasn't hearing Lara so much as *feeling* her, feeling her fury, her despair, her resolution.

Jane's eyes were shining as they met his. "That's *beautiful.*"

"It really is."

Beautiful was too weak a word. It was almost terrifying. In that instant, Ellery believed Arti. Believed that Lara was fully capable of carrying out a kind of operatic revenge on the man she believed had failed her. But that emotional force was almost too great to be directed at a single person. The singer of that song was ready to go up against the universe—and even odds on who would win such a match.

For the length of the entire song, Ellery and Jane stood silent, sharing the experience.

Then the song ended on a note of piercing sweetness, Lara fell silent, and the audience overhead erupted in muffled but thunderous applause. The spell was broken. The band launched straight into the next number.

Jane expelled a shaky breath. "Well!"

"Congratulations," Ellery said.

"Yes. Thank you." Jane blinked at him in sudden unease. "What are you doing here?"

"I was going to ask you the same question."

"Lara invited me to come backstage."

Before the performance? That was different. But Ellery said, "Well, I'm glad I caught you. I've been hoping we could chat."

Jane's expression grew more wary. "About what?"

"You knew September, didn't you?"

"No. Not really."

Ellery changed tack. "That's funny. Dylan said September had trouble making friends. You were one of the only people who gave her a chance."

All right, maybe Dylan hadn't put it quite that way, but that's how Ellery chose to interpret his words.

Jane hesitated, conceded, "We spoke sometimes. I-I felt sorry for her. I know what it is to be treated like an outsider on this island."

"It's not fun," Ellery admitted.

Jane gave him a look of derision. "You're not an outsider. You're a Page. Your family has been here as long as the Pirate Eight. Even if people didn't like you, they'd still feel you belonged here."

"Did you know her from before?" That was a total shot in the dark. He wasn't even sure why he asked.

The question caught Jane off guard. "Of course not," she said quickly, defensively. And then, "Before what?"

Ellery hadn't expected to hit gold. He said at random, "Before either of you moved to the island."

"That's ridiculous. Where would you get such an idea?"

She wasn't looking for an answer. She was preparing to beat a retreat. Ellery said, "I'm worried about Dylan, so I'm throwing stuff at the wall, hoping something sticks. I don't really know what to ask."

She frowned, but seemed to accept his explanation.

Ellery asked, "Did September ever confide in you?"

She shrugged. "Perhaps."

"Did she ever tell you she was afraid of someone?"

Jane hesitated. "No."

The hair rose on the back of Ellery's head. He realized she'd considered casting suspicion on Dylan but, for whatever reason, decided against it.

"Do you have any idea why she was so insistent Dylan include her in any meetings with Lara Fairplay?"

Jane hesitated again, but her desire to show she was in the know, warred with her sense of caution. "I think they had known each other at one time."

"Really?"

"September was a singer as well as an actress. I think they worked together a long time ago."

"That's news. I guess it makes sense. She seemed to have trouble finding work."

"She wasn't interested in finding work. If she hadn't been stupid..." Jane didn't finish the thought. Instead, she said, "Aren't you going to ask me how I happened to find the Foster fragment? I'm sure Nora is dying to know."

"I don't care about the Foster fragment."

Jane's eyes narrowed.

"Do you know who killed September?" Ellery asked.

"Chief Carson arrested Mr. Carter."

"Dylan didn't kill September."

"Then I really don't know who could have done," Jane said.

Ellery regarded her steadily. Jane stared back, but her expression grew defensive. "I don't know why you're giving me that look. I don't know! *I* certainly had nothing to do with it."

"Maybe not, but I *know* you know more than you're saying."

"You can think what you like."

"If you do know who killed her, or if someone even *thinks* you know, you could be in a lot of danger, Jane."

Jane bristled. "I could say the same to you, Ellery!" She scurried away down the hallway.

The walk back to the Crow's Nest felt endless.

He was not alone. Lots of people were coming and going on the road leading to Pirate's Cove. Many of the festival goers had enjoyed a few too many beverages, which occasionally turned the walkway into an obstacle course.

It was unexpectedly chilly and the various aches and pains of the day had caught up with Ellery, but the continued silence from Jack was what really hurt.

By the time he reached the bookshop, it took all his energy to collect Watson, bundle him into the car, and start the million-mile drive back to Captain's Seat.

In fact, it was not even twenty minutes before he pulled into the circular drive, parked, and staggered around to unsnap Watson from his harness. Watson hopped down, shook himself, tags jangling noisily, and darted off to make sure every bush and tree was as he'd left it.

Ellery crossed the broken flagstones—were these something he could afford to replace with part of his financial windfall?—and unlocked the fortress-like front door.

The familiar scents of old wood and new varnish greeted him. He'd forgotten to leave a lamp on, and the entry hall was dark. Ellery felt around for the wall switch and dazzling light from the newly rewired chandelier illuminated the cathedral ceiling, tall staircase, and the open-mouthed wooden cannons carved into the balustrade overhead.

The mansion had been built back in the 1700s by Ellery's famed pirate-hunting ancestor, Captain Horatio Page. Once upon a time, Captain's Seat had been one of the island's showplaces, but time and tide had taken their toll. With Jack's help, Ellery had been working to restore the house to a semblance of, at least, livability, and together they'd managed to make a surprising amount of progress. But to restore the mansion to its original glory would take a lot more time and a lot more money.

Although fifty grand would certainly help.

Watson, apparently under the impression the drawbridge closed at midnight, came racing through the open door behind Ellery, and skidded across the polished wood floor.

Despite his weariness and mounting depression, Ellery chuckled. "Did you almost miss your bus?"

Watson, looking a little sheepish, picked himself up, and wagged his tail.

"I think we could both use a midnight snack."

Unlike Ellery, Watson had had all his meals that day, but he still thought that was a terrific idea. He trotted into the kitchen after Ellery.

Ellery fixed Watson a small portion of his food and then opened a can of soup for himself.

Campbell's clam chowder was probably enough to get him drummed off the island in disgrace, but he was too tired to bother fixing himself anything more substantial.

He carried his bowl of chowder into the dining room, listened to the wind picking up, the scratch of branches against the windows. Forlorn sounds.

The knot in his stomach felt the size of Buck Island.

He could not seem to think past...

Well, he could not seem to think.

His brain felt cluttered with all the bits and pieces of information he had collected over the past twenty-four hours, but the puzzle was not taking shape. He was exhausted. That was a lot of it. He'd had one hell of a day.

And, of course, he was distracted, worried about the situation with Jack. Twice he picked up his cell to phone. Twice he laid his phone down. Disturbing Jack at work in order to discuss problems in their relationship was not going to win points.

Tired as he was, Ellery knew if he tried to go to bed, he'd spend the next few hours tossing and turning. Instead, he turned to his tried-and-true method of calming his nerves and focusing his thoughts: Solitaire Scrabble.

There was something soothing, centering, about playing against himself.

It wasn't just about relaxation, though. Solitaire Scrabble was a way to analyze and work through his problems without consciously trying to do that very thing. Time and time again, the words that popped up during this mental exercise were illuminating, enlightening.

It had been weeks since he'd resorted to Scrabble. Unlike those first months after he'd moved to the island, Ellery no longer had endless time on his own. But as he set up the board and tiles on the dining table, he found comfort in the familiar ritual.

He picked seven random tiles from the soft green bag and placed the first tile in the middle square on the center of the board.

He got THEN (seven points) but THEN, to his bewilderment, was stuck. And remained stuck. He struggled for time, certain that he was after AUTHENTIC, and eventually realized he was so out of practice—or perhaps so distracted—that he was looking at the board the wrong way. In fact, he had the letters for AUTHORITY (15).

It was still a miserable showing and the board was a mess of half-hearted attempts.

What the heck?

Something about that stern vertical line of tiles struck home. He recalled Nora's and Kingston's efforts to get him to see the situation at Dylan's from Jack's point of view. What they had *not* said, what only occurred to Ellery now, was that he had directly, if inadvertently, challenged Jack's authority that morning. Not Jack's authority as Ellery's boyfriend. Jack's authority as the Chief of Police.

Ellery's stomach did an unhappy flop.

Just as he had been hurt and offended that Jack would pull rank on him, Jack had no doubt been equally offended that Ellery would, well, take liberties. Ellery too had pulled a kind of rank by expecting Jack to do his job the way his boyfriend wanted, rather than the way he thought best.

Ellery could not seem to tear his stricken gaze from that single forbidding strip of letters.

Oh hey. And right next to it was IDIOT (six points).

You got this, genius!

Into these cheerless thoughts came the solemn chime of the doorbell.

CHAPTER SEVENTEEN

Ellery knocked his chair over and nearly fell over Watson in his hurry to get to the front door. He didn't bother to look through the porthole, just slid the metal bars, and yanked open the door.

The light from the hallway outlined Jack. He had changed out of uniform. In fact, it kind of looked like he had gone home to bed before receiving an emergency phone call. His brown hair was ruffled; his chin stubbled. He wore jeans and the sheepskin coat Ellery hadn't seen since the previous winter.

"Hi." To his chagrin, Ellery's voice wobbled.

"Hi." Jack smiled fractionally, though his eyes remained grave. "Still mad at me?"

Ellery shook his head, moved aside for Jack to enter. "I could ask you the same thing."

Further conversation had to wait until Watson finished hailing his hero.

ARF. ARF. ARF.

Watson's bark held a reproachful note.

Jack squatted down and Watson leapt into his arms, frantically licking Jack's chin and nose. Jack closed his eyes and endured.

Ellery smiled faintly as he watched. "Watson's going to choose you in the custody battle."

Jack's eyes opened. He flicked Ellery a quick, doubtful look. "Don't even joke."

He rose, and Watson jumped out of his arms to race down the hall ahead of them, as though to say, "This way, gents!"

Ellery asked tentatively, "Are you hungry?" His heart was beating with relief and hope.

"I could eat something," Jack admitted.

As Ellery led the way to the kitchen, he said, "You know, me getting socked wasn't even your fault."

He wasn't looking at Jack, so he couldn't see his expression, but Jack's tone was rueful as he answered, "It was *kind of* my fault. I should have tried to deescalate the situation. I lost my temper."

"I did, too." Ellery glanced back and met Jack's eyes. "I'm sorry."

"Me, too."

"I can see from your standpoint that it was all getting...a little out of hand."

Jack seemed to look inward, and if he was seeing what Ellery was—Dylan bouncing around like Harold Lloyd or Jerry Lewis—no wonder his mouth twitched.

Remembering Nora and Kingston's attempts to explain Jack's side, Ellery admitted, "It didn't help, my being there. I didn't expect you to show up."

Instead of answering, Jack asked, "How's the hunt for contractors going?"

Okay, well, maybe Jack was right. Maybe they would be better off just playing it normal, steering away from the topic of Dylan's arrest, at least for the time being.

"I've got an army of people showing up to give me estimates on Monday."

Monday was usually game night. It seemed unlikely Dylan would be in the mood for drinks and Scrabble this week. Ellery considered that for a moment. Dylan was such a central member of the community—certainly of Ellery's community—it was hard to picture life in Pirate's Cove without him.

"Ellery." Jack's tone was awkward.

Ellery opened the refrigerator and gazed at the contents. He had not been spending a lot of nights at Captain's Seat lately, and the vegetables and fruit looked a little rough around the edges.

He tried to keep his tone neutral. "He doesn't have a motive, Jack."

"Motive is subjective. You know that. September's murder wasn't premeditated. Her killer used a weapon of opportunity. He didn't go there intending to kill her. She must have said or done something that so enraged him—"

Ellery turned to face Jack. "That he'd grab a hammer and hit her from behind? Does that sound like Dylan to you?"

"I can tell you from years of working homicide that ninety percent of the crimes I investigated were not—in the opinion of family and friends—within the perpetrator's nature. *Out of character.* That's from the people who knew them best."

Ellery said shortly, "Maybe you put a lot of the wrong people in jail."

Jack opened his mouth, closed it, and gave Ellery a level look.

"That was totally uncalled for," Ellery said. "I apologize."

He could tell Jack agreed, though Jack said neutrally, "Believe me, I know you're upset. And you believe Dylan."

"I know that you're the expert, Jack. I know you have years of experience and knowledge. I respect that. I respect *you.* But I do believe Dylan. I one hundred percent believe him when he says he didn't and wouldn't kill her."

"He's been a good friend to you."

Yes. When everyone else in Pirate's Cove had seemed to believe Ellery was capable of murder—twice!—Dylan had been a staunch ally.

"That's not why I believe him," Ellery said. "I believe him because the idea that he'd kill September doesn't make sense. What could September possibly have said that would have driven Dylan to kill her? She was already badmouthing him all over the village. No one believed her. So, it couldn't have been the threat of blackmail. They weren't married. He wasn't tied to her. She couldn't take him for everything he's worth. So she didn't pose a financial threat. He wasn't jealous of her. He was *tired* of her. If she threatened to leave him or he caught her with someone else—and who would that be, by the way?—he wouldn't have been so out of control with rage that he grabbed a hammer. It. Doesn't. Make. Sense."

Jack took a moment to answer, "That will be for a jury to decide."

"He has nothing to gain from her death and had nothing to lose by her being alive."

"She owed him a lot of money. We're talking thousands of dollars."

Ellery responded, "How does killing her get him his money back?"

Despite their best efforts, their voices were starting to rise. Watson whined softly, looking from Ellery to Jack.

Jack exhaled a long breath. He said evenly, "This is why it's probably better if we don't discuss this particular case."

"Sure," Ellery said. "I don't want to fight with you. That's the *last* thing I want. But this is the thing on my mind. This is what I'm going to be focusing my time and energy on. You want to talk about the weather? Go for it."

Jack blinked as though he was seeing Ellery clearly for the first time.

And Ellery... Ellery realized that they were teetering on a very steep precipice.

He said shakily, "I'm sorry, Jack. I want to support you. I do support you. Always. But I think you're wrong about this."

He was relieved—and surprised—when Jack stepped forward, folding his arms around him in a hug that felt kind and protective. "I *know*. You're a good and loyal friend. It's one of the things I love about you. I don't want you hurt, that's all. But I'm not going to ask you to choose between... friendships. Just..." His voice dropped, his breath warm against Ellery's ear, "Don't hate me for having to do my job."

Ellery moved his head in negation. "Never."

Jack kissed his ear, let him go, and Ellery moved away to busy himself cooking a nourishing midnight supper for a nice guy who'd had a tough day.

He drank a cup of tea and Watson slept with his head on Jack's foot as Jack ate his omelet of bacon, cherry tomatoes, chives, mozzarella, and frozen peas.

Other than compliments to chef, Jack didn't say much, and Ellery stuck to the safe topics of home renovation, bookshop business, and Lara Fairplay's close call the evening before.

"*Another* near accident?" Jack put his fork down.

Ellery had assumed Jack had heard about the trapdoor incident, but of course, Jack had his own actual cases to deal with.

"It seems like a lot," Ellery agreed. "But it's not the first time there was a problem with that trapdoor."

"I still don't buy it."

"Unfortunately, the door was immediately boarded-up. So at this point I don't think anyone would be able to tell if it had been tampered with. They didn't just seal the trap door. They added a whole additional underlayer of planks and boards to the stage. I'm not sure that door will ever be operational again."

"Who gave the orders to board up the trap door?"

"I couldn't get a straight answer. Lara's road crew led the effort, but it sounded like everyone from the stage hands to sound guys were down there within seconds. If she'd fallen through—"

"That woman's got more lives than a cat."

"She's spending an awful lot of them in Pirate's Cove."

Jack took a bite of omelet, chewed reflectively, swallowed, and said, "Elon did time for embezzlement."

Ellery nearly dropped his teacup. "Say what?"

"He's got a prison record."

"When and how?"

"This was very early on. Before he got into the music business. Right out of college, he worked in the accounting department of a telecommunications company. Over the course of three years, he managed to divert assets through credit card fraud and check alteration to the tune of two hundred thousand dollars."

"Whoa."

"He was sentenced to twenty-three months, got off after fourteen for good behavior, and started his own company managing musical talent. Once he met Lara, he dumped his other clients and focused solely on her and her career."

"Did any of his other clients complain of financial irregularity?"

"Nope. But—I figured you'd find this interesting—when Lara got out of prison, she hired a financial forensics firm to run an audit for her."

"Wow. But they didn't find anything?"

"No. Everything was in order."

Ellery considered this new information. "She really doesn't trust him."

"Not with her wallet."

"Maybe not with anything. According to Arti Rathbone, Lara's big hit, 'Fool Me, Fool You,' was written about Neilson."

"I don't know the song."

"Basically, it's about a woman who out cons her conman boyfriend."

"I see."

"And maybe Lara's right not to trust him. Her sister, Jo, said Neilson used to fool around on Lara. Her version is, Lara didn't care about that. But she did say when Lara went to prison, she got paranoid and changed her will. Lara didn't feel that Neilson had fought hard enough to keep her from going to jail."

"Hm."

"Jo said Lara changed her will back after she got out. But I spoke to Lara on Friday morning, and Lara indicated she *hadn't* changed her will back. Her sister's the sole beneficiary."

"Interesting."

"Lara also mentioned her estate wasn't worth what it was before she went to prison."

Jack thought it over. "What about life insurance?"

"That goes to the kid sister, too."

"What's the relationship between the husband and the kid sister?"

"Cozy," Ellery said promptly. "I'm not saying there's anything going on between them—Jo seems loyal to her sister—but she's definitely fond of Neilson."

"That's two viable suspects right there—and both are on-scene."

Ellery studied Jack. "Thanks for digging that information up, Jack. You didn't have to."

"No, I didn't have to. But I knew you were worried."

Even if Ellery had still been angry, still been blind to his responsibility, his role in escalating the trouble between them to downright turmoil, Jack's words would have melted his heart.

Ellery stretched his arm across the table, and Jack immediately linked fingers with him.

Later, when they were tucked up in bed, beneath the slightly askance painted gaze of Ellery's ancestor, Captain Horatio Page, Jack murmured, "How's your chin?"

Ellery said wryly, "Still wagging, as you see."

Jack made a soft sound of amusement. "I'm sorry." He nuzzled Ellery behind the ear. "Really, truly sorry."

"I know. Me, too."

"I couldn't *believe* it when I realized I'd hit you." There was a faint echo of the note of horror Ellery had heard when Jack's fist connected with his chin.

"Me neither." But Ellery could almost smile about it now. Even Jack's stricken expression was sort of funny in hindsight.

Watson, as if following their conversation, clambered over Ellery's back and gave the chin in question a snuffling inspection.

Ellery started to laugh, turning his head. Jack muttered, "Hey you. Quit horning in on my action."

Apparently satisfied with the state of Ellery's face, Watson circled a couple of times and settled on the pillows between their heads. He grunted, like a little old man easing into his rocking chair, tucked his nose beneath his tail, and eyed Jack without blinking.

Ellery laughed again, this time at Jack's expression.

"Okay, I get the message," Jack said.

"Nah. He's Team Jack all the way."

They smiled into each other's eyes.

Ellery said reluctantly, "Jack, I'm going to help Dylan any way I can."

"I know."

"If that means amateur sleuthing—"

"I know what it means."

"I hope you can understand."

"I understand." Jack said wearily, "Do you really think if you and the Silver Snoops uncovered evidence to send this investigation in another direction, I wouldn't be glad? Relieved?"

Ellery started to ask, *would you*? But he knew the answer to that. Yes. Jack would be relieved, glad, happy, you name it.

"Just don't make it personal," Jack said. "Because it isn't personal for me. It's my job."

Ellery said carefully, "Maybe it should be personal, though."

Jack didn't answer right away, and Ellery knew he was as reluctant as he to shatter their fragile peace. "Is this about Dylan or is this about you and the Abbott case?"

Ellery did a quick bit of soul searching, and admitted, "Maybe it's both."

"That's what I was afraid of. Listen, I explained my reasons then."

"Yep. You did."

"And I stand behind them now."

"Oh, I know you do."

Jack's face colored. He pushed up on elbow. "You know, just a reminder: I didn't enjoy that either. Any of it. I didn't like seeing you interrogated, treated like a suspect. I didn't like hearing that *Thanks, friend.* It wasn't easy to see that look on your face, and know what you thought. I sure as hell didn't enjoy you believing I'd betray our...our friendship."

"I don't think you enjoyed it, but you were willing to do it."

"Yes. I was. It's my *job.*"

Ellery started to speak, but Jack cut him off. "Also, I explained at the time why it was in *your* best interest that I made damn sure to maintain every appearance of propriety and objectivity. The same's true in Dylan's case. If it looks like I'm pulling strings and protecting my friends, this thing will hang over him forever."

Ellery sat up. "Jesus, Jack. Maybe you're right. I'm sure you *are* right. But sometimes, *sometimes* you really need the reassurance of knowing your friends believe in you!"

Jack sat up too, their knees resting against each other beneath the sheets.

"I did believe in you." Jack looked as troubled as Ellery felt. "I came to you and *told* you I believed you."

That was true. No doubt against his better judgement, Jack had come to Ellery and tried to explain himself. Tried to reassure Ellery that he didn't believe he had committed murder.

And that had meant a lot to Ellery.

He said sincerely, "I remember. And I do understand. But I can't pretend it didn't hurt. A lot. Especially because I really, *really* liked you, Jack. And you'd already made it clear you didn't feel the same. So, your friendship was all I had." Embarrassingly, his voice shook.

Jack's face twisted, and he pulled Ellery to him. "But I did feel the same. I *do* feel the same. I do really, *really* like you, too. You know I care for you. You know I...I wouldn't deliberately hurt you. Not ever."

Ellery nodded, said into Jack's bare shoulder. "I know. And despite what it sounds like, I'm okay with it. I'm good. It's just this particular situation dredged up some stuff I thought was over and forgotten."

Jack's hands closed on Ellery's shoulders, pushing him back a bit so they could read each other's faces. "Maybe that's not such a bad thing because it seems like you *aren't* completely okay with it. I don't want there to be any misunderstandings or doubts between us. I'm not a robot. I can't just switch off my feelings. I try to give what the job demands; I know I don't always get it right. But I never want to get it so wrong that you believe I'm not on your side. Or that I'm not going to be there for you."

That was as close as Jack had ever come to making a commitment, and it did ease a lot of the old angst and uncertainty.

Ellery nodded. "I believe you. And I'll remember that the next time it feels like we're on different sides."

"Try to remember this," Jack said. "We're *not* on different sides."

Ellery meet Jack's gaze and felt a flicker of surprise. But yes, of course, Jack was absolutely right. Ultimately, they both wanted what was best for their friends, their community, and, maybe especially, for each other.

He smiled. "I won't forget." He reached for the lamp.

CHAPTER EIGHTEEN

Miss Pinky called the council,
to see what they could do.
She didn't live through two world wars,
to have PIRATES spoil her view!

When Ellery arrived at the Crow's Nest on Sunday morning, Kingston was sitting on a large rug in front of the bay windows, reading from a picture book to a small circle of very young children.

Watson opened his mouth to protest the unauthorized use of floorspace designated for chasing balls and rubber chew toys, but Ellery scooped him up and carried him off to the sales desk where Nora stood beaming.

Ellery whispered, "I didn't realize we were starting the storytime thing this weekend."

"No time like the present." Nora pressed the bell on the old-fashioned cash register which popped open to offer Ellery a view of a lot more dollar bills than were typically there on a Sunday morning.

"Eighty smackeroos," Nora informed him. "If we served coffee, it would be double that."

"If we served coffee, we'd be cited for not having a food service license. I thought storytime was going to be on Saturdays?"

"It will. This is just a trial run. The music starts later on the second day of the festival."

"It's fine with me. That's a very nice rug. Where did it come from?"

"Kingston purchased it for story time."

"Kingston bought it? With his own money?" Ellery bit his lip. "I need to reimburse him."

"No, dearie. It's Kingston's gift to the bookshop."

Ellery whispered, "Kingston shouldn't be giving the bookshop gifts when the bookshop might not be able to keep him on."

"Now, now. Let's keep a positive attitude."

Ellery opened his mouth, and Nora added, "I suspect Kingston would like to continue Saturday Storytime even if you can't afford to employ him."

"Really?" Ellery gazed doubtfully at the rapt circle of children.

> *They never wash.*
> *Their kids have lice.*
> *They really don't smell very nice.*

Kingston's audience began to giggle and roll around on the carpet.

"He's really *very* good," Nora murmured approvingly.

Watson, who'd seen enough of this nonsense, raised his head to object, but Ellery nodded hastily to Nora and carted him off to his office.

He set Watson on the floor, closed the door, and sat down behind his desk. He turned on his computer, but his smile was not for Yahoo's bleak presentation of world events. Despite being worried about Dylan and Lara Fairplay, he was feeling happy, even contented.

Somehow, he and Jack had managed to weather the kind of rough weather that would have sunk any of his previous romantic relationships. The variable had to be Jack. Ellery was not kidding himself he'd suddenly learned the secret to making relationships work. He was learning not to duck conflict. It was still hard sometimes to trust that this relationship wasn't going to end like all his relationships, but he was getting better about communicating both what he feared and he what he wanted. And that was because of Jack. Because Jack was so honest, it was easier to return that honesty.

One of the things I love about you.

Ellery had not missed those casual words the evening before. He knew it wasn't a declaration. Knew Jack had used the phrase the same way Ellery intended when he said he loved old movies or Chinese food or Broadway shows. In the very same breath Jack had said, *I'm not going to ask you to choose between...friendships.*

No, Ellery didn't want to make *too* much of that little lone word, even though it seemed he'd been waiting an awfully long time to hear it. But he couldn't help feeling the sun was shining a bit more brightly that morning.

He became aware that Watson was sniffing loudly beneath the bottom of his office door. Sniffing and muttering beneath his breath. Watson was not a fan of children, possibly because kids had a tendency to try to pick him up by parts of his anatomy not intended for use as a handle.

To distract him, Ellery opened his desk drawer, felt around for a new unopened toy, and instead felt the unfamiliar shape and texture of something square and flat in a thin plastic bag.

He drew out a green plastic bag encasing a square envelope and stared.

Through the plastic he could make out the words
ELLERY PAGE

How the heck had he forgotten about this?

For a few seconds he studied the crude writing.

Was it good news or bad news to know he wasn't the only
person in the world getting hate mail from Buck Island?

But realistically, how many authors of poison pen letters
could be running around Pirate's Cove?

Jack could probably quote him statistics.

*I can't help thinking that sending a warning to someone
you intend to kill is merely making your own life more difficult.*

Nora had a point.

Okay, once again from the top: who stood to gain from
Lara's death?

Not the festival organizers. Not Pirate's Cove. Not Buck
Island. *Maybe* Dawn Shumway's family would get some
satisfaction out of Lara's demise—it didn't sound like it—
but as far as practical, substantial gain? Jocasta and Neilson
were the most likely contenders.

Jocasta for sure.

If Neilson wasn't in Lara's will and wasn't collecting
Lara's insurance money, it was hard to see what he had to
gain by her death. Not as her husband, but what about as her
business manager?

If Lara was dead, was it possible the value of her back
catalog would rise?

Probably. But again, wouldn't Jo be the one reaping the
benefits?

Ellery was missing something. He could feel it. There
was another angle. What? Neilson was a pragmatist. If he
was going to kill his sole client, he'd have a strong, *practical*
reason.

But was there any good, as in *practical,* reason to send threatening letters to someone you intended to kill?

Yes.

To create the illusion that a crazed stalker was after Lara. So that if something happened to her, the conclusion would be her stalker got her rather than the obvious suspects?

Did that make sense?

On the one hand, it established the idea that an outsider wished to harm Lara.

But on the other hand, it gave Lara a heads up. It gave Lara's road crew and security people a heads up. It had prompted the festival organizers to hire someone to find out who was behind the threats. It had alerted the local police. And while Lara had refused to involve the local police, if something *did* happen to her, the police would certainly investigate.

So how useful a ploy was it?

Yes, Lara had had two close calls over the course of the weekend, but in each case those close calls had been put down to accidents. If it hadn't been for the anonymous threats, it was doubtful anyone would be thinking much beyond Lara was very lucky/unlucky (depending on how you looked at it) and the Loon Landing Boathouse needed to be retired as a performance venue until it could be overhauled top to bottom.

If you planned to kill someone and make it look like an accident, was there any rational reason to send death threats ahead of time?

Ellery couldn't think of one.

Which meant?

The death threats were not connected to Lara's accidents.

Maybe Lara's accidents really *were* just accidents.

But if they were *not* accidents...

Ellery mulled that over for a minute or two, then bundled Watson back into his harness, picked up the envelope in its baggie, and exited his office.

He held up the plastic baggie, mimed to Nora that he was going out, and Nora gave him a thumbs up.

> *...and there to her amazement*
> *was a CROSS on every lawn!*

The door to the Crow's Nest firmly closed, swallowing the rest of it.

* * * * *

"Did someone deck you?" Lara asked when Ellery joined her at her breakfast table a few minutes later.

"Sort of. It was an accident." Ellery declined Jocasta's offer to order him food, but accepted a cup of tea.

Jocasta poured the tea as Ellery, wearing gloves, carefully drew out the envelope, opened it, and showed Lara the card.

I'M GOING TO KILL YOU!!!!! read the childish-looking writing.

"Does this look familiar?" Ellery asked.

Lara looked surprised and then thoughtful. "This was addressed to you?"

"Yes."

Jocasta, who had taken the seat beside Ellery, sucked in a breath and said, "It looks exactly like the letters Lara's been getting. Same paper. Same writing. It's even the same message as the last one."

"Is it?" Lara asked blankly. She studied the card, shrugged. "You've seen one death threat, you've seen them all."

"Are you sure it's the same?" Ellery asked Jocasta.

"Positive."

Not exactly science, was it? "Is Neilson around?" Ellery asked. "Could he take a look at this?"

"He's over at the festival grounds," Jocasta said.

Ellery bit his lip. "Okay. Thanks." He picked up the card, slid it back into the envelope, stuck the envelope back in the plastic baggie, and departed.

* * * * *

An hour later, Ellery walked into Pirate's Cove very small, *very* quiet police station.

It wasn't his imagination, right? Everyone seemed to be tiptoeing around the building.

Ellery was ushered into Jack's office by the same youthful female he'd witnessed getting chewed out the evening before. She closed the door on him with the air of a zoo keeper serving a tiger his first course.

Jack looked up. His eyes looked very blue in his unexpectedly stern face.

Unexpectedly stern, because Jack had been in an excellent mood when he'd left Captain's Seat that morning.

"Hey," Ellery said.

"Hey."

As Ellery approached the desk, his gaze fell on the copy of the *Scuttlebutt Weekly* lying on Jack's desk blotter. The banner headline read, A RUSH TO JUDGEMENT?

Uh oh.

Following his gaze, Jack remarked, "It seems you're not alone in feeling I should've held off charging Dylan."

"Oh hell. Jack."

"It's fine. It comes with the territory."

"I'm sorry. Anyone who knows you, knows you're—"

"It's okay." Jack was brusque. What did you need?"

Ellery held up the green baggie. "I showed this to Lara and Jocasta. They think it's the same."

Jack made no move to take the plastic bag. "They think it's the same *what*?"

"They think their death threats were written by the same person who's sending me threats. They think we have the same poison pen pal."

Jack's brows knotted together. He opened his desk drawer, pulled out a pair of black nitrile gloves, and took the envelope from Ellery. He drew out the envelope, removed the letter inside, and silently read I AM GOING TO KILL YOU!!!!! without expression.

"Fairplay determined hers came from the same author based on eyeballing your letter? She didn't keep her own letters, correct?"

"Right. Correct. I know it's not forensic proof, but this isn't about prosecuting anyone."

Jack's brows drew together. "It sure as hell needs to be."

"No, I *mean*—what I'm getting at it is, I don't think the person who sent these threats to Lara is behind her accidents. There might be something prosecutable here—" Catching Jack's eye, Ellery amended, "I'm *sure* this is something prosecutable here, but it isn't attempted murder." Jack started to reply, and Ellery added quickly, "*But* I also don't think Lara's accidents are accidents. I think someone's definitely trying to kill her."

Jack studied him, said—and it was not a question, "The husband."

"Too obvious?"

"It's only the least likely suspect in books and movies."

"Well, it could be the sister. I lean toward the husband. But actually, right now, I'm just dealing with the writer of these letters. And I think I know who it is."

"Who?"

"Imelda Appleby."

Jack blinked. "The receptionist at Vincent Veterinary Hospital?"

"Yes."

"Have you ever had any problems with Imelda?"

"No. None. Never. She's always very pleasant. Actually, she's a really good customer."

"Has Lara ever had any problems with Imelda?"

"She'd never even heard of Imelda."

"Then why…"

"I don't know." Ellery shook his head. "No clue."

"Then why do you think Imelda is sending you death threats?"

"I guess she doesn't like me."

"Right," Jack said patiently. "What is the *basis* for your belief that Imelda is the one leaving you death threats?"

"*Oh.* She dropped off a box of used paperback books late Friday. Then Saturday morning, I found this envelope at the bottom of Rupert's case. I forgot about it until this morning, but then, when I started thinking about it, I realized that these letters always seem to show up after Imelda's been by the store."

Jack looked less impressed than Ellery had hoped. "You're saying *every* time Imelda visits the store—"

"No. But—I think—every time a letter is left, Imelda has visited the store."

Jack opened his mouth to point out all the obvious flaws in this sort of deductive reasoning, but Ellery said triumphantly, "*Plus*, she was caught on the security cameras."

That clearly startled Jack. Ellery smiled. "You can see for yourself. I emailed you the CCTV footage."

Without a word, Jack turned back to his computer monitor, and checked his email. A couple of clicks later, he murmured, "So you did."

Ellery waited, doing his best to remain patient, as Jack downloaded the video and opened the file. "You'll want to start watching around timestamp four forty-five."

Jack wheeled his chair to the side so Ellery could watch with him. Ellery couldn't help thinking that the a.m. scents of coffee and shower gel were especially appealing on Jack.

"Here's where I leave to go meet you for dinner," he commented.

They watched his tall figure walk through the bookshop. He paused at the door, called something to Nora, who was out of frame, stooped to pat Watson, and stepped out of the grainy video.

Watson threw his head back and began to soundlessly bark.

"You can see there's no envelope on Rupert's case." Ellery glanced at Jack's freshly shaven profile. "Now, at five to five, Kingston leaves and here comes Imelda."

Sure enough, at five minutes to five, Kingston held the door for Imelda Appleby lugging a cardboard box of paperback books. She waved off Kingston's attempt to take the box. Kingston departed. Imelda carried the books up the aisle and out of frame.

"You can't see on this camera, but on the other camera, Imelda and Nora chat for about seven minutes. If you fast forward... Right. At this point, the Crow's Nest is officially closed. Nora goes to put Watson in his crate and Imelda leaves. Watch..."

They watched as Imelda's diminutive figure bustled down the center aisle. At the front door, she paused, glanced furtively back in the direction of the sales desk, and slipped something white out of her purse. Quick as a flash, she propped the white envelope on the base of the glass case, and went out, carefully, quietly closing the door behind her.

Jack glanced at Ellery.

Ellery said, "You can fast forward again. Nora doesn't notice the envelope when she leaves. And I don't notice it when I come to pick up Watson at about six-thirty."

In silence they watched Ellery re-enter the bookshop. He freed Watson from captivity, then, moving at the speed of a character in a silent film, chased him around the store— Watson bouncing up and down like a large black rabbit.

Jack snorted.

Finally, Ellery caught Watson and buckled him into his harness.

The white envelope was still propped at the foot of the display case as Ellery turned out the lights and went out the door with Watson.

Jack swiveled his head, meeting Ellery's gaze. His expression was flinty.

"Thank you for insisting I install those security cameras," Ellery said.

Jack grunted.

"I have no idea why, but it looks to me like Imelda's writing poison pen letters in her spare time."

"Everyone needs a hobby." Jack was not smiling though.

"I feel bad because I always sort of wondered in the very back of my mind if Jane was leaving me those letters."

"Jane? Jane Smith? Why?"

"I don't know. Paranoia? But then I don't know why Imelda would leave these letters either. And something about Jane's has always been sort of secretive." Ellery shrugged.

"All right," Jack said briskly. "Leave this to me. I'll bring Imelda in and hear what she has to say."

That sounded like a dismissal to Ellery.

He moved away from Jack's desk, saying, "Okay. Thank you." He headed for the door.

Jack said, "Wait a sec. Have a seat. I was just about to phone you when you showed up. I have information that might be helpful to you."

"Really?" Ellery took one of the chairs in front of Jack's desk.

"It turns out September St. Simmons was a stage name."

"That makes sense."

"September's real name was Sybil Simon. It turns out Sybil did time in federal prison for extortion and blackmail."

Ellery absorbed that, and said quickly, "There's no way she was blackmailing Dylan. Dylan's life is an open...stage. He'd never put up with someone trying to blackmail him. He'd never pay a dime in blackmail money."

Jack smiled faintly. "I agree. I don't think she was black-mailing Dylan."

"You *agree*?"

Jack nodded, "Yes. Dylan was paying her rent, but that had nothing to do with extortion and everything to do with sleeping with her."

"Who was she blackmailing?"

"There's no evidence she was blackmailing anyone. She was financially strapped. The only checks she deposited were from Unemployment and the rent money from Dylan. Without Dylan's help, she couldn't have afforded to contin-ue to live on the island."

"Hmm." Ellery considered this new lead. Once a black-mailer, always a blackmailer? If so, September AKA Sybil didn't appear to be very good at it. "It turns out I have infor-mation that could be useful to *your* case. According to Jane, September knew Lara from back in the day. Jane was a little vague on the details, but it seems September claimed that at one time she had performed with Lara."

"What did Lara say to that?"

Ellery scratched his nose. "To be perfectly honest, I sort of forgot Jane told me that until just this minute."

Jack blinked. "You *forgot*?"

"It's not like I do this for a living. The last couple of days have been kind of a lot."

"Right. Is there anything else potentially helpful to my case you might have forgotten?"

"If I remember I'll let you know."

Jack stared at him without blinking.

"I'm kidding," Ellery said. "Obvi."

Jack shook his head.

A thought occurred to Ellery. "Were there any finger-prints at the scene."

Jack regarded him, then said dryly, "Tons of latent fin-gerprints. I assume you mean usable prints?"

"Right."

"Not so far. The crime lab is still processing, seeing if they can come up with something that could be run through AFIS."

PICO PD did not have its own crime lab. When it came to forensics, they were dependent on the mainland.

"Okay."

Jack sighed. "If we come up with anything, I'll let you know." His gaze dropped automatically to the newspaper on his desk.

Ellery said, "Just one more thing."

Jack looked up. He raised his brows. "Yep?"

"Will I see you later?"

Jack's mouth twitched into a half-smile; his eyes softened. "Of course."

Ellery leaned over the desk, brushed Jack's mouth with his own, and went out, carefully closing the door.

CHAPTER NINETEEN

Dylan and Janet were still in their bathrobes, having breakfast when Ellery arrived at Janet's cottage shortly after leaving the police station.

It was barely eleven o'clock. Ellery accepted coffee, declined a slice of Quiche Lorraine, and sank into a pillowy chair cushion in the cozy living room.

Ellery's relationship with Janet had been rocky to start with, but over the past months they had grown more cordial. He sort of liked her acerbic wit—when it wasn't directed at him—and she was a *very* good Scrabble player, so high praise indeed. He'd never been able to quite figure out Janet's relationship with Dylan. They were clearly good friends. At one time, he'd suspected they were more than friends, but Dylan always denied it, and Janet had most recently been dating Tom Tulley, owner and proprietor of the Salty Dog.

That said, they were cozy as two peas in a pod that morning, sitting beside each other on Janet's cabbage rose floral chintz sofa. Dylan still looked tired and pale, but he was not nearly as haggard as he'd been the previous day.

Very possibly Sue Lewis's fierce defense of him in her editorial for the *Scuttlebutt Weekly* had provided some comfort. The paper was lying open on the coffee table.

Sue and Dylan went way back, but Ellery couldn't help thinking Sue was taking the opportunity to vent some of her private frustrations with Jack in a public forum. It was very much her modus operandi.

Ellery took a swallow of tea and winced.

Dylan also winced. "How's your jaw, kiddo?"

"It only hurts when I laugh."

Janet snorted. "You're lucky you don't have a black eye. Who would have dreamed Jack Carson would turn out to be an abusive boyfriend?"

"*Hey*," Ellery said in warning.

Janet gave an evil laugh.

Dylan began to mutter dire things about police brutality.

"Okay." Ellery put his coffee cup down. "I want to help, but I'm not going to listen to you two shred Jack."

"I'm afraid, after my incarceration, I can't be as forgiving," Dylan said huffily.

Ellery didn't bother to point out Dylan's incarceration had only lasted about forty-five minutes and Jack had even forborne adding the charge of resisting arrest. Dylan had been through a painful and humiliating experience. He had a right to be upset.

"No, I know. And I don't agree with Jack arresting you, but the Washington County DA had a say in that. It wasn't all Jack's choice. Lansing is the lead detective."

That didn't seem to carry much sway with Dylan or Janet, so Ellery moved on to other topics. "Dylan, did you know September was a convicted felon?"

Janet did a doubletake. Dylan, a forkful of quiche headed to his mouth, froze. "She *what*?" He put down his fork.

"She went to prison for extortion and blackmail."

"Good God in Heaven."

"Why am I not surprised?" Janet remarked to no one in particular.

Dylan's expression was bleak. "I had no idea. Maybe that explains why she didn't have much to say about her past, why she didn't seem to have any friends or family."

"Well, that's something I wanted to ask you. Aside from you, was she close to anyone in Pirate's Cove?"

"No.

"No one at all?"

"She tried," Dylan said. "I think she wanted to fit in."

"I don't," Janet said.

Dylan looked pained. "She could be insecure sometimes."

Janet raised her brows, but said nothing.

"What about within the theater group? Was she close to anyone in the Scallywags?"

"Not really."

Janet said, "September waltzed in believing that she was going to be the most beautiful, talented, and popular actress on the island. She had a rude awakening when she ran into Libby Tulley."

Dylan looked even more uncomfortable. He said suddenly, "Jane Smith. They were friendly." He grimaced. "Although September looked down on Jane."

"Naturally," Janet said.

"But I think Jane was the closest to a real friend."

Ellery nodded, stared at the newspaper on the coffee table. "Is it possible she could have been seeing someone else?"

"No, no," Dylan said at once.

Janet was clearly biting her tongue.

Dylan added bitterly, "She wouldn't jeopardize her meal ticket."

Ouch. Ellery had no idea what to say to that. He suspected Dylan was right.

Dylan glared at Ellery. "I suppose Jack imagines September's criminal past gives me an even greater motive for murder."

"I don't think so. He said to me, *you might find this helpful*. He knows I'm going to do everything I can to help clear your name."

"Bless you, Ellery." Dylan reached across the table and gripped Ellery's hand. "I know that, too."

"I have another question, but this is unrelated to your situation."

"Anything I can do to help," Dylan assured him.

"Does the Sing the Plank festival have insurance?"

Dylan looked confused. "Insurance? Of course."

Janet said, "Do you mean, are the performers insured?"

"I mean, if a performer is killed on stage because of a faulty trap door or a falling light fixture, what happens?" He already knew the answer, but he needed to verify.

"The family or record label or management company would almost certainly sue the festival. And if it can be proven festival organizers breached their duty to take reasonable safety measures, the injured party would collect a large chunk of change."

"How large a chunk of change?" Ellery asked.

Dylan frowned. "If we're talking about Lara Fairplay, and I assume we are, somewhere north of a million dollars."

Jocasta phoned as Ellery was scrunching behind the wheel of his Volkswagen.

"Hi! I don't know if this is helpful or not, but I just saw the newspaper."

Not incredibly helpful, but okay.

"Oh?" Ellery prompted.

"We'd heard about Mr. Carter's girlfriend, but we didn't actually watch the news or anything. Lara won't have the TV on or newspapers lying around. She doesn't like that energy."

"No news is good news, I guess."

"Exactly. Anyway, I *do* like to look at the newspaper sometimes, and I was reading your *Scuttlebutt Weekly* this morning."

"Right, right." Ellery tried to control his impatience.

Jocasta exclaimed, "I know her! I knew her."

"Who?"

"Sibyl. Well, I guess she was calling herself September. She was one of Lara's backup singers a long, long time ago."

"You knew September when she was Sibyl Simon?"

"Yes. This was at least fifteen years ago. I was still a kid, but I remember. She wasn't with us for that long. She went to prison for trying to extort money from a married record producer she'd slept with."

It took two tries to get Jack.

On the second try, Jack picked up, sounding slightly harassed. "Hey, can I call you back? I'm in the mid—"

"Yes. Just really fast. Fifteen years ago, Sibyl Simon was a backup singer for Lara Fairplay. I think she slept with Neilson Elon during that time and I think she was trying to extort money from him. I think it was Neilson she was expecting that night. Not Dylan. I think Neilson killed her."

Jack said crisply, "Okay. I'll call you right back."

"*Wait*! Jack. There's more. I think Neilson really is the one trying to kill Lara. I think he's been trying to arrange a fatal accident during one of her performances, so his music company can sue the festival."

"Okay, Ellery. Let—"

"Lara's last performance is at one, Jack. I think Neilson is over there right now sabotaging that stage."

Ellery ran out of breath and words about the same time.

There was a moment of silence, then Jack said, "I'm on my way. I'll radio ahead and get some officers into that building. You don't need to go over there."

"Right."

"You're going over there, aren't you?"

"Yes."

"Ellery—"

"Jack, I know theaters. I know stages. I can be of help."

Jack made a sound of frustration. "I'll be there in seven minutes. Don't go in that building without me."

"I'll wait. I promise."

"See you in six-point-five minutes." Jack hung up.

* * * * *

Ellery hadn't tried driving over to the festival before, so it took longer than he'd expected to find the area a distance from the food and entertainment designated for parking.

He climbed out of the VW and started across the grassy field to the Loon Landing Boathouse Theater.

There was a decent crowd milling around the souvenir booths and small stages. Four different bands competed for airspace and listeners.

To his relief, he spotted Officer Martin and two other uniformed members of PICO PD jogging toward the landing.

Whoooo.... Whooooo.... WHOOOOO!

As Ellery passed the amateur stage, a familiar and alarming wail caught his attention.

It was not the sound of approaching police cars however.

Nor an ambulance.

Nor the scream of Pirate's Cove's Fire Department trucks come to save the day.

Nope. These unearthly cries were accompanied by the earnest *twang* of a banjo and plaintive *plink* of a ukulele?

He turned to see Nora and Kingston standing on the stage, singing for all they were worth.

> *Blow, ye winds in the morning,*
> *and blow, ye winds, high-o!*
> *Clear away your running gear,*
> *and blow, ye winds, high-o!*

The crowd obligingly joined in on the chorus. Nora and Kingston beamed at each other.

Ellery glanced back at the landing and saw Neilson coming out through the tall doors of the boathouse. He was talking with Olive Earl, one of the Sing the Plank committee members. Olive was nodding and smiling.

It all seemed pretty benign, and Ellery felt a twinge of unease.

It was going to be awkward if it turned out Neilson had simply been going over the stage map with the lighting tech.

But as he watched, Neilson looked away from Olive, and caught sight of the approaching officers.

Officer Martin recognized Neilson, spoke to his uniformed companions, and then pointed at their target. It wasn't subtle.

Nor was it subtle when the three officers started running toward the boathouse.

Maybe it was guilt. Maybe it was instinct. Maybe it was the natural reaction to three people shouting and running toward you at full speed that made Neilson turn and bolt, but bolt he did.

He raced for the golf cart parked at the side of the boathouse and threw himself into the driver's seat. He started the golf cart which began to bump and bounce its way across the grass.

Neilson beeped the horn frantically as he dragged the wheel left and started toward the meadow. The trio of officers ran a little way after him, then slowed to a walk, then came to a stop.

The buzz of the golf cart faded as the cart grew smaller in the distance.

Ellery turned as Jack jogged up. "I don't know where he thinks he's going."

Jack's grin was sardonic. "Not far. That's for sure."

In silence they watched the golf cart slow as Neilson tried to jerk and yank his way through the tall grass and mud of the soggy marshland. The engine's whine grew higher, higher, as the cart went slower, slower...and eventually fell onto its side.

CHAPTER TWENTY

"**Y**ou were partly right," Jack said. "Elon deliberately re-moved some of the grounding from the sound system. All Lara would have had to do was grab the mic while she was holding her guitar, and it would have been all she wrote."

It was long after midnight on Sunday night. Ellery and Jack were sitting in front of the fireplace in the front parlor at Captain's Seat, having a late-night drink. The cheerful fire, the first of the autumn season, cast playful light over the old portraits and faded furniture.

"*Partly* right?" Ellery echoed, holding his brandy snifter away from Watson's curious inspection.

"He was trying to kill her. No question in my mind. Elon's fingerprints were on the cable that supposedly snapped when that PAR can light fell on Friday night. There's only one explanation for his prints being up there. He tampered with the cable."

"You checked the rigging for fingerprints?" Ellery was impressed. It hadn't occurred to him fingerprints could be recovered.

"I know," Jack said. "It's like I think I'm a cop or some-thing."

Ellery spluttered a laugh, then asked, "Did he confess?"

"Nope. He's exercising his right to keep his mouth shut. Which is wise."

"Is out on bail?"

"No. The soon-to-be former Mrs. Elon has no interest in bailing him out. She seems to be in no doubt as to his intentions."

"Poor Lara."

Jack nodded, but said, "She didn't seem too broken up about it. The kid sister was crying her eyes out."

Ellery threw him a curious look. "You said I was only partly right. What part did I get wrong?"

"Elon didn't kill September."

Ellery sat up straight, dislodging Watson who had just settled against him. "He *had* to have."

"He didn't do it. He has an alibi for the time in question."

"Jack, Dylan didn't—"

"Stop," Jack ordered, and Ellery stopped. But the relief that had buoyed him through the afternoon and evening had evaporated.

"Dylan didn't kill September," Jack said.

"Oh thank God." Ellery let his head fall back on the sofa. "Thank *God*." He studied Jack's profile in the firelight. "Does Dylan know?"

"Dylan knows the charges have been dropped."

Ellery couldn't quite read Jack's tone. "So... Are things okay between you two?"

"No. Dylan says it will be long time, if ever, before he can forgive me." Jack shrugged.

"I'm sorry."

"No need. It's nothing to do with you."

Jack was stoic, but Ellery knew him well enough to know losing Dylan's friendship had hurt him.

Ellery frowned. "But if Nielson didn't kill September, who did?"

"Odds are good she was killed by Judith Stockton."

"Who?"

Jack's smile was arid. "We were able to lift several partial prints at the crime scene. We ran them through AFIS and got a hit."

"AFIS is the fingerprint database?"

"The Automated Fingerprint System. It's only useful if you're trying to match prints that are already on file. In this case we were and they were. In this case, we were able to match the prints to Judith Stockton."

"Who the heck is Judith Stockton?"

"Judith Stockton was—still is, I guess—a small-time document forger. She went to federal prison for forging passports and green cards. For a short time, she was Sibyl Simon's cell mate."

"Jane Smith." Ellery stared at Jack in consternation. *"Jane?"*

Jack met his gaze gravely.

"But…"

"But?"

"You're serious?"

Jack nodded.

"But why? Why would she? Have you questioned her? What did she say?"

"She hasn't said anything because she left the island last night."

"She— She's on the *run*?"

"That would be my best guess." Jack half rose, picked up his jacket and drew out a long, white envelope. "See what you think."

Ellery took the envelope. His name was neatly written across the front. "She left me a letter?"

"Yep."

"You read it?"

"It's evidence. Yes."

Ellery lifted the flap, pulled out the single sheet of paper, and began to read.

Dear Ellery,

The jig is up. I realized tonight that you know the truth. I knew you were getting close, but I thought I had a little more time. At least I got the pleasure of hearing my greatest work brought to life. It's fitting, I think, that you were there to share my achievement.

Jack said, "Did you know the truth?"

Ellery shook his head. "I mean, it went through my mind—but it kept going. I couldn't see that Jane would have any motive. I didn't even remember to ask her what she was doing skulking around Lara's hotel suite on Saturday. I still don't know what that was about."

He resumed reading.

I hope you believe me when I say, I didn't mean to kill Sibyl. It wasn't an accident, but I didn't go there intending to do her harm. I asked her, for old time's sake, not to ruin my setup by trying to black-mail Neilson. Sibyl was not a smart woman—she was probably the most selfish person I've ever known. She brushed off my concerns, and when I told her how hard I'd worked to arrange the purchase of the Foster fragment, she told me what I wanted was not important. That I was not important.

It was not a surprise to me. Sibyl never pretended she thought anyone was as important as she. I was there when she left that phone call for Mr. Carter.

It made me sick. She was always cruel. It wasn't deliberate. It's just how she was. And for some reason, when she picked up that cocktail tray and went sashaying off—so sure that he was going to come running—I decided it was time for her to go.

Ellery looked up. Stared at Jack. "Yikes."

"You can say that again."

I was sorry when Mr. Carter was arrested, but that couldn't be helped. It will be all right now.

I would like you to know that I had more fun this last year than all the years I lived in Pirate's Cove. That is mostly because of you. I hope you have a long, happy life with Chief Carson. And I hope you see the light, eventually, and fire Nora.

Best regards,

Jane Smith

Ellery blinked. "What made her think I'd figured it out?"

"Your reputation precedes you?"

"Ha. Not so much. It's kind of alarming how much fingerprints and forensics had to do with solving both these cases."

"I know," Jack sympathized. "I'm sure from your perspective it feels like cheating."

"Pretty much." Ellery sighed sadly.

He was a terrible actor, and Jack shook his head and stretched his arm out. Ellery shifted Watson onto his lap, and scooted over. He rested his head on Jack's shoulder. He felt Jack's quiet laugh and turned his face up for Jack's kiss.

"Did you have a chance to talk to Imelda?"

"*Oh.* Yeah. That's who I was dealing with when you phoned about Nielson."

"I assume she denied everything?"

"Actually, no. She fainted."

Ellery's eyes popped open. "She *fainted*?"

"Yep. I guess getting caught was a big shock."

"Were you able to talk to her at all?"

"Not really. She did say it was all a misunderstanding."

"How so?"

"She's not planning to kill you or anyone else. She just felt it would do you good to be taken down a peg. Her exact words."

"Taken down a peg?"

"I guess you're getting too large for your britches, Mr. Page."

"What about Lara?"

"Imelda felt Lara should have done the tasteful thing and retired after getting out of prison."

Ellery absorbed this latest news. "So... Is that it?"

"No."

Ellery regarded Jack's for a moment. Jack was staring at the fire. He lowered his gaze. His eyes met Ellery's.

Watson raised his head, looked from Ellery to Jack, and yawned so widely, his jaw squeaked.

The corner of Jack's mouth tugged into a faint smile.

"It'll wait," Ellery agreed.

AUTHOR'S NOTE

Dear Reader,

Welcome back to Pirate's Cove, that quaint, cozy seaside village where secrets spread like wildflowers, the phrase *family bloodlines* has a whole new meaning, and a colorful cast of characters are prone to uttering the occasional New England colloquialism like...*snum*. (Yep, it's a real word. Look it up.)

The Secrets and Scrabble series is set on fictional Buck Island, which is sort of a blend of Block Island and Catalina Island. The character of Watson is based on my own lunatic adopted pup Spenser (*né* Watson).

If you have little seafarers in your crew, you might be interested in the book Kingston chooses to kick off the first Saturday Storytime: *The Pirates Next Door* by Johnny Duddle.

Thank you to my editor Jennifer Jacobson. Thank you to Kevin for the endless cups of iced coffee and runs for fast food. Thank you to the Office Elf.

Thank YOU, dear readers. I could not make this voyage without you.

ABOUT THE AUTHOR

Author of 100+ titles of Gay Mystery and M/M Romance, Josh Lanyon has built a literary legacy on twisty mystery, kickass adventure, and unapologetic man-on-man romance.

Her work has been translated into twelve languages. The FBI thriller *Fair Game* was the first Male/Male title to be published by Italy's Harlequin Mondadori and *Stranger on the Shore* (Harper Collins Italia) was the first M/M title to be published in print. In 2016 *Fatal Shadows* placed #5 in Japan's annual Boy Love novel list (the first and only title by a foreign author to place on the list). The Adrien English series was awarded the All-Time Favorite Couple by the Goodreads M/M Romance Group. In 2019, *Fatal Shadows* became the first LGBTQ mobile game created by *Moments: Choose Your Story*.

Josh is an EPIC Award winner, a four-time Lambda Literary Award finalist (twice for Gay Mystery), an Edgar nominee, and the first ever recipient of the Goodreads All Time Favorite M/M Author award.

Josh is married and lives in Southern California with her irascible husband, two adorable dogs, a small garden, and an ever-expanding library of vintage mystery destined to eventually crush them all beneath its weight.

Find other Josh Lanyon titles at www.joshlanyon.com

Follow Josh on Twitter, Facebook, Goodreads, Instagram and Tumblr.

ALSO BY JOSH LANYON

NOVELS

The ADRIEN ENGLISH Mysteries
Fatal Shadows • A Dangerous Thing • The Hell You Say
Death of a Pirate King • The Dark Tide
Stranger Things Have Happened • So This is Christmas •

The HOLMES & MORIARITY Mysteries
Somebody Killed His Editor • All She Wrote
The Boy with the Painful Tattoo • In Other Words...Murder
The 12.2-Per Cent Solution

The ALL'S FAIR Series
Fair Game • Fair Play • Fair Chance

The ART OF MURDER Series
The Mermaid Murders •The Monet Murders
The Magician Murders • The Monuments Men Murders
The Movie-Town Murders

BEDKNOBS AND BROOMSTICKS
Mainly by Moonlight • I Buried a Witch
Bell, Book and Scandal

The SECRETS AND SCRABBLE Series
Murder at Pirate's Cove • Secret at Skull House
Mystery at the Masquerade • Scandal at the Salty Dog
Body at Buccaneer's Bay • Lament at Loon Landing
Death at the Deep Dive • Corpse at the Captain's Seat

OTHER NOVELS

This Rough Magic • The Ghost Wore Yellow Socks
Mexican Heat (with Laura Baumbach) • Strange Fortune
Come Unto These Yellow Sands • Stranger on the Shore
Winter Kill • Jefferson Blythe, Esquire
Murder in Pastel • The Curse of the Blue Scarab
The Ghost Had an Early Check-out
Murder Takes the High Road • Séance on a Summer's Night
Hide and Seek

NOVELLAS

The DANGEROUS GROUND Series
Dangerous Ground • Old Poison • Blood Heat
Dead Run • Kick Start • Blind Side

OTHER NOVELLAS

Cards on the Table • The Dark Farewell • The Dark Horse
The Darkling Thrush • The Dickens with Love
I Spy Something Bloody • I Spy Something Wicked
I Spy Something Christmas • In a Dark Wood
The Parting Glass • Snowball in Hell • Mummy Dearest
Don't Look Back • A Ghost of a Chance
Lovers and Other Strangers • Out of the Blue
A Vintage Affair • Lone Star (in Men Under the Mistletoe)
Green Glass Beads (in Irregulars) • Blood Red Butterfly
Everything I Know • Baby, It's Cold (in Comfort and Joy)
A Case of Christmas • Murder Between the Pages
Slay Ride • Stranger in the House • 44.1644° North

SHORT STORIES

A Limited Engagement • The French Have a Word for It
In Sunshine or In Shadow • Until We Meet Once More
Icecapade (in His for the Holidays) • Perfect Day
Heart Trouble • Other People's Weddings (Petit Mort)
Slings and Arrows (Petit Mort)
Sort of Stranger Than Fiction (Petit Mort)
Critic's Choice (Petit Mort) • Just Desserts (Petit Mort)
In Plain Sight • Wedding Favors • Wizard's Moon
Fade to Black • Night Watch • Plenty of Fish
Halloween is Murder • The Boy Next Door
Requiem for Mr. Busybody

COLLECTIONS

Short Stories (Vol. 1)
Sweet Spot (the Petit Morts)
Merry Christmas, Darling (Holiday Codas)
Christmas Waltz (Holiday Codas 2)
I Spy...Three Novellas
Dangerous Ground The Complete Series
Dark Horse, White Knight (Two Novellas)
The Adrien English Mysteries Box Set
The Adrien English Mysteries Box Set 2
Male/Male Mystery & Suspense Box Set
Partners in Crime (Three Classic Gay Mystery Novels)
All's Fair Complete Collection
Shadows Left Behind

SPECIAL EDITIONS

Fatal Shadows: The Collector's Edition

Printed in Great Britain
by Amazon

23134525R00136